"What have you done with her?"

Chris's voice shook. "Where's Colette?" As he stared down the barrel of his captor's large gun, Chris felt a searing rage surge through him, driving out all other emotions.

He'd been lured to this spot by Colette's frightened voice—only to find himself caught in a trap.

This was the second attempt on his life in one day. The first time he'd been rescued by an anonymous phone call, but out here in the middle of nowhere he was strictly on his own.

And where was Colette? Had she fallen into their clutches as well, or was she part of their insidious plot?

Other

MYSTIQUE BOOKS

by ROBERTA ROLEINE

For a free catalogue listing all available Mystique Books,
send your name and address to:

MYSTIQUE BOOKS,
M.P.O. Box 707, Niagara Falls, N.Y. 14302
In Canada: 649 Ontario St., Stratford, Ontario N5A 6W2

Storm over Ibiza

by ROBERTA ROLEINE

MYSTIQUE BOOKS

TORONTO • LONDON • NEW YORK
HAMBURG • AMSTERDAM

STORM OVER IBIZA / first published February 1980

ISBN 0-373-50067-X

PRINTED IN U.S.A.

Chapter 1

Chris Laval shrugged his collar up around his ears, lowered his head and stalked grimly through the wind-whipped drizzle. He couldn't recall spring being this cold and damp in Barcelona. As he negotiated a narrow, cobblestoned street made treacherous by the fine rain, he silently cursed himself for succumbing to the nostalgic glow of his earlier visit to Barcelona instead of asking his travel agent what sort of weather to expect. A chill was settling over him, creeping into his shoulders and making his legs ache. And this denim outfit was the warmest thing he'd brought. Damn! He'd probably freeze on Ibiza, as well.

Chris's dark thoughts expanded to include the taxi driver who had politely insisted on dropping him off in front of the government buildings, "several short blocks" from his destination. Much as he would have liked to carry the young *señor* to the door of the *casa* de Charraca, the driver had explained with a smile, he couldn't possibly take his automobile beyond San

Jaime Square. The streets of the Gothic section were impossibly narrow. Surely the young *señor* understood...?

No, Chris didn't understand. But after a solid week spent marking his students' term papers, the long flight from Paris had left him without the energy to argue. The driver had obviously sized him up and dismissed him as just another *turista*. With an unhappy sigh, Chris had paid the fare shown on the meter and set out with his suitcase in the rain.

The streets weren't that narrow, Chris thought glumly as he glanced around him. Then he amended his judgment as he turned onto a winding lane where the buildings fronted directly on the road, leaving no room for a sidewalk. Worn smooth by countless generations of feet, the rain-slicked cobblestones made simple walking a dangerous adventure. Maneuvering a car could be an impossible mission.

Suddenly, once again, Chris had the eerie feeling that he was being watched. Quite different from the crawling discomfort of being exposed to a needle-like rain, this was a subtle anxiety that sat twitching in the pit of his stomach, a sensation Chris had been living with for several weeks now. He already knew what he would find when he whirled to scan the street behind him, but he turned anyway. The lane was deserted. Beneath the overcast sky everything looked dull and gray.

Chris sighed wearily. He was no great fan of mystery novels, and he especially hated to see his neat, well-ordered life dissolving into one. When it had dawned on him, weeks ago, that he was being systematically observed, he had naturally sought an explanation. If the watcher was a burglar, intending to rob Chris's apartment during his absence, the fellow had already missed several prime opportunities. But who else might have a reason to follow his every move?

Chris had racked his brain, trying to wring some obscure detail out of his memory that might explain why he'd been placed under surveillance. But his status as a landed immigrant in France had never been questioned, he had no police record in France or Canada, he didn't smoke pot or dabble in illegal activities of any kind. Chris Laval had never so much as defaced an old poster.

He even *looked* like an innocent. In a moment of desperation he'd stepped in front of a mirror one day, thinking there might be something suspicious about his appearance. But the gray eyes that had gazed back at him were direct and friendly, while the expression on his angular, slightly irregular face had been pure bewilderment.

There was probably just a misunderstanding, he'd told himself hopefully. Eventually the mistake would be discovered and rectified. Back home in Canada Chris would simply have marched into the nearest police station and demanded to know what was going on. But a North American colleague at the University of Paris had warned him how touchy and difficult the European authorities could be. Perhaps when he'd built up some seniority at the university he could gamble on a confrontation. Meanwhile, without tangible proof that he was being followed, Chris would only get himself branded as an oddball.

So for nearly five weeks Chris had waited patiently for the error to be sorted out—waited patiently and in vain. And now here he was in Barcelona, still being shadowed! Yielding to an angry impulse, he yelled into the empty street, "Get lost, you creep!" Then he turned and resumed his search for the *casa*.

There were many imposing mansions in this oldest section of Barcelona, but their beauty was dulled, not only by the weather but by air pollution. It was the bane of all industrialized nations: white buildings looked gray; gray buildings looked dingy. Any other color was barely discernible beneath a layer of grime.

The fine ocher facade of the *casa* de Charraca had palled in the translucent shroud of smoke that hung in the air. Still, it was an elegant old house. Its arched lintels and mullioned windows were decorated with fine wrought-iron grillwork. Over the main portal hung a coat of arms surrounded by foliated scrolls, with the household motto engraved beneath the crossed swords of the emblem: *Antes de todos, ante todos, encima de todos*—before all, above all, upon all. It was a startling show of pride even for Spaniards—a traditionally proud people.

The sculpted oak door was wide open. As Chris strode through the portal he heard a polite voice behind him. "Admission to the museum is fifty *pesetas, señor.*"

"Museum?" Astonished, Chris glanced across the courtyard toward the main building, whose severe lines were softened by a row of fluted balconies and an intricately sculpted stone cornice. "Isn't this the *casa* de Charraca?"

"Yes, sir, it is," replied the porter carefully. A short, wiry man with prominent veins in his forehead, he wore the neutral expression universally assumed by guards and watchmen.

"The home of Count Esteban de Charraca?" Chris went on.

"Ah! You wish to see the count?" At Chris's nod, the guard continued, "You'll have to go to the private residence, sir. The entrance is just around the corner."

Feeling mildly irritated, Chris went back the way he'd come. Granted, Esteban had never discussed his financial position, but he *had* described this mansion and had used such superlatives to describe its elegance and luxury that Chris had naturally pictured it filled with scurrying servants and the music of one gala reception after another. A museum! Surely Esteban could have mentioned that small detail to him when he'd invited Chris to spend his Easter vacation with him in Spain!

Count de Charraca was one of Europe's foremost authorities on North African civilizations, and an anthropologist of world renown. He and Chris had first met at a series of lectures Esteban had agreed to give at the University of Paris the previous summer. Newly arrived to take up his teaching post with the Romance Languages Department, Chris had wandered in on one of Esteban's talks while trying to orient himself.

Tall and spare, with a shock of thick black hair and a stern, weather-beaten face, the count was a striking figure. His passionate interest in his work also made him an arresting speaker. Chris had lingered, enthralled, at the back of the lecture hall until the hour was up, before coming forward to introduce himself.

Despite a gap of eleven years in their ages and the differences in their backgrounds, the two men had hit it off immediately. At first Chris had been merely flattered at the Spaniard's interest in him, assuming that it would peter out once de Charraca was back at his dig in Ibiza. But then Esteban's letter had arrived, marking the beginning of an absorbing, eight-month-long correspondence. Chris had accepted with alacrity the count's invitation to spend Easter week with him in Barcelona and then at his dig. He felt privileged that this reserved Spanish nobleman had singled him out as a friend.

From the street Esteban's private residence looked like any other smallish house, and Chris experienced a pang of regret as he knocked at the door. He felt vaguely as though he were about to expose a charming fraud, or restore Don Quixote to lackluster sanity. Even though Esteban hadn't pretended to be very wealthy, his title and the home he'd described had created an illusion of opulence—an illusion Chris would rather have kept intact.

Just then the door was opened by a fragile-looking woman in her sixties, wearing a long black skirt with a yellow sash. Her gray hair had been plaited and then pinned in coils at the nape of her neck, and her face was finely wrinkled. "Yes?" she said, frowning at the tall, rangy stranger in blue denim as though he'd just stepped off a spaceship.

"I'm Christopher Laval," he said almost apologetically.

Suddenly her dark eyes lit up. "Of course, the Spanish professor from France!" she cried, and swung the door wide for him. "Come in, come in!" As he gratefully stepped out of the rain, she commented in a motherly voice, "But you look so much younger than I was expecting."

"That's because I'm not a full professor," he explained. "I'm only an associate professor."

The woman shrugged and shook her head dismissively. "It doesn't matter what they call you," she declared. "You still look too young."

Amused, Chris followed her into the count's private residence. Esteban hadn't lied about the richness of its furnishings—the decor showed a Spaniard's predilection for leather and brass, with here and there a lingering Eastern influence revealed in the colorful carpeting, the several tasseled throw cushions on the divan and the occasional brocaded chair. Reds and browns dominated the color scheme in the living room, the drawing room and the guest suite, which the elderly servant placed at his disposal "for as long as he remained under the count's roof." It would be a short stay, Chris reflected, since he and Esteban were to catch a boat that very evening for Ibiza.

"Where is Count Esteban?" Chris asked.

The servant's welcoming smile faltered momentarily. "The count is unable to greet you personally. He left a letter for you," she explained, pointing to an envelope propped against a bowl of fruit on a lovingly-polished pine table next to the window. "I am Rosita, the count's housekeeper. If you need anything, please call me." And with that she was gone.

Chris picked up the letter and sank down on a surprisingly comfortable red- and gold-brocaded chair to read it. Glancing out the window he saw the iron railing of a fluted balcony and realized with a start why the small house seemed so spacious inside—it was actually one wing of the *casa* de Charraca.

Esteban's handwriting was sloppy, and Chris felt

like an archaeologist deciphering hieroglyphics as he read:

My dear friend,
Please accept my deepest apologies for not waiting for you, but there is an emergency on Ibiza
requiring my immediate presence there. Make
yourself at home in the *casa* for the several hours
before the boat sails. Rosita is a warm and obliging
person who will do everything she can to make
your stay pleasant. I'll be waiting for you when
the boat docks in Ibiza. Bon voyage!

Chris heaved a sigh, abruptly aware of his bone-
weariness. He'd arisen at five that morning to pack,
then sat through delay after delay at Paris's Orly
Airport before his flight to Barcelona finally departed,
hours behind schedule. Counting all the waiting he'd
done for various reasons at both airports and the time
spent getting to the *casa* by cab and on foot, Chris had
been in transit for almost eleven hours. He felt tired
and chilled. If only there were time for a long, refreshing sleep before he had to resume his travels. . . .

Suddenly there was a knock at the door. "Come in,"
he called, and Rosita appeared, carrying a tray.

"We dine late, usually," she explained, busily setting a place for him on the table by the window. "But I
couldn't help noticing how cold and wet you looked
when you came in, so I fixed you a snack."

Chris thanked her and gazed appreciatively at the
plate of sandwiches and pastries and the huge pot of
steaming coffee in front of him.

"It's only four o'clock," Rosita continued. "You
don't have to leave for the docks for another two

hours, so once you've eaten you'll have time to walk through the museum if you wish. Perhaps on your way out?"

"Sounds great," he agreed with a smile.

She nodded. "Call me when you're ready to go, then, and I'll let you through the connecting door."

Chris resisted the temptation to linger over the coffee, which was strong and very rich. Once he'd disposed of the sandwiches and sampled some of the pastries, he downed his third delicious cup and headed for the washroom with his shaving kit.

Chris had made one abortive attempt to grow a beard during his undergraduate days, but his whiskers had come in fiery red, jarring so painfully with his light blond hair that he'd looked and felt like a freak. Now each time he shaved, he repressed a regretful sigh, for a beard would have tempered the often embarrassing youthfulness of his face. His eyebrows were so pale they almost disappeared against his fair skin, giving his dark-lashed gray eyes a saucerlike look of perpetual naiveté, while his smile was naturally lopsided—"boyish" was the term used by a girl he'd tried unsuccessfully to impress back home. Perhaps his upcoming thirtieth birthday would make a significant change in his life . . . ? Chris grinned ruefully at himself in the mirror. He could dream.

The door to the museum stood at the end of a hallway running between the dining room and the kitchen.

"I'm going to lock it tight behind you," Rosita advised, showing him her ring of large, old-fashioned keys. "In this weather I'm sure there can't be many people here, but it only takes one intruder . . . ." She didn't have to finish her thought—the foreboding

expression on her face presaged barbaric plundering.
"You must leave the *casa* at six o'clock, six-twenty at
the latest," she went on. "Hernan, the porter, will tell
you how to reach the docks. Have a pleasant voyage,
señor professor."

"*Gracias*, Rosita."

The old woman shrugged uncomfortably. "*De na-
da.*" she muttered, closing the door between them.

The de Charraca mansion made an excellent
museum, Chris decided, with its random arrangement of immense, richly appointed rooms and its fine
collection of Spanish art masterpieces. The furniture
here was much older and more graceful than the
heavy leather pieces in Esteban's apartment, although
no less tasteful for being a purposeful display of
wealth. Wandering through an elegant salon and a
solemn dining room into a second parlor just as
sumptuous as the first, Chris admired the bold orien-
tal colors and sinuous Arab motifs in the carpeting, in
the tapestries that adorned the walls and in the
brocaded fabrics that covered divans, chairs and windows. Each detail spoke loudly of Esteban's past, for
in its way the *casa's* interior was as prideful as the
motto over the gate.

Chris was apparently the only visitor. It was
exhilarating to stand amid such splendor, and he
wished he could spend a whole day exploring it, but a
glance at his watch told him that he had less than half
an hour before he had to leave. The second salon
opened onto the main entrance hall of the *casa*. He was
making his way to the front door when he heard the
sound of a door clicking shut behind him. *That's funny*,
he thought. *I could have sworn I was alone here.*

Curious, he deposited his suitcase on the floor near

the entrance and made his way to the door that had just been closed. He thought that there was a suite of rooms beyond it.

Halfway there he froze, as he strained to identify the noises that had stopped him so suddenly in his tracks. Chris had heard—or thought he heard—footsteps in the next room, silenced by an urgent "Sssh!" These might be ordinary visitors feeling intimidated by the grandeur of the mansion, but somehow Chris doubted it.

He glanced around quickly. The museum seemed suddenly cold and very still. For a second he toyed with the idea of going outside to fetch the porter, then he dismissed it. He was probably being too fanciful. He didn't *know* that anything was amiss.

Cautiously Chris made his way across the dining room and eased open the door a few inches, permitting a view down one bare wall of the adjoining room. Nothing. Just then a male voice hissed, *"Pronto,* Dolores! Hurry!" Chris heard a tearing sound, then the dry crunch of breaking wood.

Telling himself unconvincingly that Dolores and her friend might be engaged in something quite innocent, Chris pressed lightly against the door and watched it swing soundlessly a little wider. Then, when this move failed to produce any reaction inside the room, he peered carefully around the edge of the door . . . and found himself staring into a pair of large dark eyes.

The girl was young, no more than twenty-two or -three, and strikingly beautiful. She had a thick fall of long black hair, a narrow Roman nose, delicately arching eyebrows and the sort of dark complexion that evoked images of the Middle East. And she was crouched on the floor, apparently unframing paintings. As his eyes traveled to the stack of canvasses beside her, the girl automatically shifted position to conceal them. But there was no way she could hide the pile of splintered frames directly in front of her.

Frowning, Chris gazed around the empty walls of the room and stepped inside for a better view. Evenly spaced at eye level he saw lighter squares where paintings must have hung. "What the hell . . . ?" he muttered, then took several threatening steps toward the girl, who held her ground, gazing serenely into his scowling face. "What the hell are you doing?" he demanded.

In that instant he realized that there should have been a man in the room with her. But it was already too late. Suddenly a beefy arm was around his throat and a strangely sweet-smelling piece of cloth was being pressed to his face. Chris held his breath as he tried to twist out of his assailant's grasp, but the choke-hold held fast. He struggled violently, his lungs starved for air, his chest aching with the need to breathe. He couldn't hold out any longer, he had to have air. He took one gulping breath and in a matter of seconds he felt all the strength drain from his body as his eyes closed and his mind spun off into darkness.

Chapter 2

Reluctantly, Chris opened his eyes. There was a throbbing all around him. The very air seemed to be picking up the vibrations and communicating them to the roaring pain in his head, with much the same effect as if he were trapped inside an echo chamber while a recording of the human heartbeat played at a hundred decibels. He hadn't been this hung over the morning after his twenty-first birthday!

Lying very still, he gradually became aware of other sensations. He was on a narrow bed whose linens had a strange, rough feel to them, a bed that was rocking back and forth like a cradle. As his memory returned in bits and snatches he recalled a pair of lovely dark eyes, a pile of broken picture frames and a desperate struggle not to inhale as a muscular arm tightened around his windpipe.... Suddenly Chris realized that this was no ordinary hangover he was experiencing.

"Damn..." he moaned, clutching his head as the pain grew momentarily worse. *Where am I?* Slowly he rolled over onto his side and maneuvered himself into a sitting position. He was in a tiny room, containing two identical wooden beds and a large sturdy dresser, all fastened to the floor, and various small accoutrements such as a wastebasket and a small rattan table secured between the two beds. Halfway up one wall was what appeared to be a shiny black circle. Then Chris took a closer look and found that it was a porthole.

His jaw dropped. He was on a boat! But what kind of boat, and going where? As the boat rocked, he became aware of a dull scraping sound coming from beneath the bed. Kneeling, he discovered that his suitcase had somehow found its way on board. Chris struggled to master the pain in his head as he opened his bag for a quick inspection. Nothing had been removed... except his ticket to Ibiza.

Torn between rage and panic, he managed to negotiate the swaying passageway and reach the deck. A near gale-force wind was whipping up waves that tossed the ship like a toy, and a uniformed crewman intercepted Chris before he got halfway to the rail.

"There's a storm brewing, sir," the sailor shouted over the wind. "You'd best return to your cabin for now."

Stubbornly Chris shook his head. "I have to see the captain," he insisted. "I think I'm on the wrong boat."

"I doubt that, sir—we're very careful about checking tickets. However, if you still want to see the captain I'll take you to the bridge."

"Please do," Chris rejoined impatiently. The sailor shrugged and turned, beckoning to him to follow. By the time they'd stepped out of the wind Chris's ears were ringing and he had to swallow hard several times to clear them, each gulp triggering a wash of pain at his temples.

Captain Castillo was an imposing, authoritative-looking man with a full black beard and a forbidding expression on his lined face. He glanced up briefly from a nautical chart as Chris and his guide entered the bridge, then returned to his calculations, muttering darkly to himself.

The sailor halted smartly in front of the chart table and cleared his throat. "Captain Castillo?"

"What is it?" the captain growled.

"This passenger has a problem, sir. He believes he's on the wrong boat."

"He does, does he?" Scowling heavily, Castillo gazed up at Chris. Then a light of recognition gleamed in the captain's dark eyes and he chuckled deep in his throat. "That's perfectly understandable," he said, his smile revealing a gold tooth near the front of his mouth. "How are you feeling, Mr. Laval? I'll bet you have quite a headache after all the drinking you and your friends did this afternoon."

Intuitively Chris stifled the impulse to correct his false assumption. After all, Captain Castillo had called him by name and provided a plausible reason for his condition. He couldn't be sure he was out of the woods just yet. Smiling feebly, Chris replied, "Yes . . . but how did you know my name?"

"It's printed on your ticket," Castillo said reasonably. Then, evidently noticing the dubious expression on Chris's face, he went on, "Your ticket to Ibiza."

"We're going to Ibiza?" Chris said incredulously.

Castillo laughed. "You see, Mr. Laval? Drunk as they were, your friends managed to put you on the right ship. We'll be docking early tomorrow morning."

Chris was baffled. Either he had just had a run-in with the most considerate art thieves in the world... or else they weren't ordinary art thieves.

"What's wrong, Mr. Laval?" asked the captain. "You look disturbed."

His mind racing, Chris replied, "Oh, er, it's just that I meant to do something before leaving port. It's... quite important. Could I send a message to Barcelona?"

"Certainly. Ferrer, show Mr. Laval to the radio room."

As the captain resumed poring over his charts, the sailor who had brought Chris to the bridge reappeared at his elbow. With a wink and a sympathetic smile he jerked his head in the direction of the door. "We have to go down one deck," he explained once they were outside. The companionway was sheltered from the gusting wind, enabling the men to talk in normal voices. "So you tied one on, eh?"

"That's the way it's beginning to look," Chris sighed, then asked guardedly, "I gather you weren't there to welcome me aboard?"

"No, I was busy loading the cargo," Ferrer explained. "But I heard about your dramatic entrance from the purser. Ah, here we are."

The radio officer was making entries in a narrow, leather-bound logbook as they walked in. Glancing around, Chris noted that the room was tidy and spartanly furnished. A row of identical logbooks stood on a console table against one wall. The operator was sitting on the only chair, in front of another table that held an impressive collection of electronic equipment.

"What can I do for you?" asked the radio officer, closing the logbook and slipping it between two metal boxes that bristled with knobs and switches.

"Mr. Laval wants to send a message to Barcelona," Ferrer announced.

The radio officer looked Chris slowly up and down. "So *this* is Mr. Laval," he commented with a smile. "You look much healthier than I imagined you."

Chris slumped wearily against the edge of the table. "Is there anyone aboard who *doesn't* know how I arrived?" he asked.

"Don't take it so hard," Ferrer said coaxingly. "This is a small vessel making a routine run. We have little else to talk about. Besides, Castillo won't allow any drinking on his ship, so we're all a little jealous of you."

"I believe Mr. Laval has a message for Barcelona?" the radio officer cut in. Chris nodded. "Write it out on this pad," he said briskly, and slid paper and a ball-point pen across the table. "We charge standard telegram rates for personal messages." When Ferrer had taken the hint and left, the officer muttered just loudly enough for Chris to hear, "If that boy doesn't learn some discretion he'll one day be the oldest midshipman in the merchant marine."

A few minutes later Chris handed the pad and pen back to the radio officer, who scanned the brief message and stared coldly up at him. "This must be some kind of joke, Mr. Laval!"

"What do you mean?" Chris asked, puzzled.

"You spend the day carousing with your friends, drink yourself into a stupor and have to be carried aboard, then ask me to send this to the Barcelona police?" Snatching up the paper he read in an incredulous voice, " 'Investigate art theft this afternoon *casa* de Charraca.' "

"It's a legitimate report," Chris said urgently. "The crime *did* take place—I witnessed it."

"Before or after you were, er, indisposed?" At Chris's stricken look, the radio officer continued in a reasonable tone, "Look, Mr. Laval, the Barcelona police wouldn't take kindly to a false alarm. You could have been mistaken, you know . . . considering everything. Besides, if what you say took place really happened, the police will already know about it. You can always contact them later if you feel you have important information. Why don't you sleep on it?"

"If what I say . . . really happened . . . ?" Chris echoed faintly. He folded the message and slid it into his jacket pocket. "Thanks anyway," he sighed, and headed back to his cabin.

Grimly Chris realized that he'd underestimated the art thieves' cleverness. They had actually rid themselves of a bothersome witness by simply sending him on his way, making him seem enough of a reprobate that nobody would take his claims seriously once he'd "sobered up." After all, how could he have witnessed a crime if he'd spent the day drinking with his friends? And how reliable was the memory of a man who had drunk himself into a stupor?

Who would believe he'd been drugged? Chris could hardly believe it himself. He was now certain of one thing, though—those were no ordinary art thieves.

Suddenly feeling as though he'd suffocate if he spent another minute in his cabin, Chris borrowed an oilskin from a passing crewman and made his way above deck.

The deck was cold and swept by ruthless gusts of

wind and spray. It was a perfect setting for the desperate thoughts that were going through Chris's mind, and he lingered at the rail for a while, mulling over all the unpleasant possibilities.

The thieves had managed to ruin his credibility temporarily, but the fact remained that he was an eyewitness to their crime. He'd got a good look at the girl and could probably pick her out of any crowd. Once off the ship, Chris would become a key witness against them. They must have realized that. So why had they let him go?

Of course they could always find him again, having personally put him aboard this vessel. It was a chilling thought. *So now I not only have my unknown tail to worry about, I also have to be on the lookout for Dolores with the dark eyes and her gorilla friend. . . .*

Suddenly there was a gentle tap on his arm. Chris jumped and whirled around, startling the young woman who had approached him. She gasped and stepped backward, giving him several seconds to take in her heart-shaped face with its wide hazel eyes and generous mouth and the wind-tangled mass of her thick, shoulder-length brown hair. Her raincoat flapped wildly in the breeze, and Chris caught glimpses of a trim young body. She looked so fresh and natural that Chris had to smile with delight. It was as though a door had opened, letting this ray of light into his darkening world.

"I'm sorry," she said in heavily accented Spanish, shouting to be heard over the wind. "I didn't mean to startle you."

After two-and-a-half semesters spent teaching at a French university Chris recognized the French accent at once. "That's all right," he replied in the young woman's mother tongue, and she gave him a charm-ing—and relieved—smile.

"I didn't *think* you were Spanish," she said. "I'm Colette Vaubois."

"Christopher Laval."

She shook her head in puzzlement. "Laval is a French name, but you have a strange accent. . . ."

"No kidding!" He laughed. "I'm from Canada. Are you interested in languages?"

"Yes, I am," she replied, smiling. "In fact I'm in my last year of Italian and German at the Sorbonne. But I began auditing classes in Spanish last September, when I made up my mind to visit the Islands. Do you enjoy conversing in shouts?" she added teasingly, and Chris took the hint and led her to a relatively sheltered place near the companionway where they could talk in normal tones. It wasn't as well lit as the open deck, but Chris found himself drawing comfort from her shadowy presence beside him and not caring over-much that he couldn't discern her finely etched fea-tures in the dark.

"So you're a student." His eyes twinkled with amusement. "Are you a good one?"

"I'm an interested one," she replied thoughtfully, missing the bantering tone. "What about you?"

Chris shrugged philosophically. "I'll probably be a student until the day I die," he mused. "There's so much to learn."

"Oh, come on!" she exclaimed indignantly. "I know exams seem to sneak up on you sometimes, and it's natural to feel a little blue at this time of the year, but the only reasons you could have for doing poorly are laziness and ineptitude. You don't look to me to be suffering from either one," she declared with finality.

Chris chuckled to himself. "Thanks for the compliment . . . I think."

"What year are you in?" she asked.

"Uh . . . this is my first," Chris replied, surrendering to his sense of mischief.

"Oh," she said in an understanding voice. "You got a late start, did you?"

Bless you, young lady, he thought as he struggled to keep from laughing.

"By the way, how's your head?" she asked solicitously. "You were in pretty bad shape when your friends carried you on earlier."

Suddenly it was as though the door had slammed shut again, dooming him to a world of shuddering darkness. For a brief moment he'd been able to forget about all the unpleasantness attending his arrival on board the ship. Now it washed over him with renewed menace.

"Did you see them?" he growled.

There was an uncertain pause. "Sure. I was on deck."

"What did they look like?"

"Like Spaniards. Dark hair, dark eyes, dark skin . . . ." Another pause, then, "But you should have known that, shouldn't you? I mean, they were your friends."

Angrily, Chris shook his head.

"What's the matter?" she asked, timidly touching his sleeve. "Are you all right?"

"It's a long story," he said brusquely, shrugging off her hand. "Please excuse me, Miss Vaubois. I have a great deal on my mind just now." Abruptly he turned and headed for his cabin.

PLACES HAD BEEN SET for breakfast in the dining room when Chris appeared at the door in soggy denims at seven-fifteen the next morning. A smirking waiter showed him to his table.

The borrowed oilskin was too short to protect his long legs, and to reach the dining room he'd had to cross the quarter deck, where twenty-foot waves smacking the side of the ship had drenched him with cold, salty spray. The sea was even rougher than it had been the previous night, causing the ship to buck and bounce sickeningly. Meanwhile, the sky overhead was leaden and threatening, a perfect partner to the bone-chilling wind that now assaulted the vessel so determinedly. Once again Chris berated himself for not having packed a coat.

"Continental or English breakfast, sir?" the waiter asked in a bored voice.

"Continental, I guess. And can you tell me when we'll be docking in Ibiza?"

"The weather has delayed us a couple of hours, sir."

"Which means?" Chris persisted.

Smiling artificially, the waiter replied, "Which means we'll be late."

Chris grinned right back at him. "I see. I'll toss a few numbers at you and you tell me if I'm close. Nine o'clock? Ten? Eleven?"

"You're warm."

"Ten-thirty?"

Sighing dramatically, the waiter declaimed, "Who can say for sure, *señor*? The ship could hit a rock and sink." And with that he was gone.

While waiting for his meal to arrive, Chris gazed anxiously around the dining room, looking for a lovely heart-shaped face framed by brown hair. His rudeness to Colette the previous night had disturbed him so much that, unable to sleep, he'd returned topside to see if she was still there. He might not have been able to explain his conduct to her, but he certainly felt he owed her an apology. Naturally, she had disappeared by that time, and Chris had had to return to his cabin.

He scanned the dining room as he ate breakfast, and once more as he was leaving, but there was no sign of Colette. Damn! He had to find that girl, and not just over a nicety of manners, but because he genuinely liked her. She'd been intelligent and easy to talk to. She'd been interested in him. She'd brought some levity into his life just at a time when he'd needed it most, and for that alone he wanted to thank her.

But she'd said she was visiting "the Islands," not Ibiza. Once they landed he might never see her again. Oh, Lord, he had to find her before the boat docked....

It was against his better judgment but Chris was desperate. He approached the waiter with a question. "Do you know one of the passengers, Miss Colette Vaubois?"

"I know many women, *señor*."

"She's fairly tall, slender, with sort of longish brown hair."

The waiter heaved a sigh. "You've described half the women of Spain, *señor*."

"Miss Vaubois isn't .... Never mind," Chris exclaimed impatiently. "Just tell me where I can find the purser."

Another question. Chris realized his mistake the moment he opened his mouth, but the words popped out anyway.

"You mean at this very moment?" the waiter asked politely.

"Of course!"

"He could be anywhere on the ship," said the waiter with a smile.

"Thanks. You've really been· helpful," Chris muttered, and hurried to catch up with another crewmember he'd glimpsed striding down the passageway.

The purser was in his office, guarding a stack of luggage that had been checked into the hold for the duration of the voyage and that he'd just spent more than an hour retrieving. He was happy to give Chris the number of Colette Vaubois's cabin and even drew him a map showing the quickest way to get to it. Meanwhile Chris was slowly becoming aware that it would have been wiser to skip breakfast, as his stomach began pitching in time with the ship.

He glanced at his watch and saw that it was nearly nine o'clock. Chris's heart sank a little. Despite the explicit instructions of the engineer's mate whom he'd accosted in the passageway, Chris had lost his way several times while looking for the purser's office, and it had taken him more than half an hour to get there. With the aid of the purser's map, he shouldn't have any trouble finding Colette's cabin. But what if she had eaten early and then decided to go exploring the ship? He might never find her.

With a growing queasiness that wasn't entirely indigestion, Chris set off doggedly in the direction of her cabin.

Chapter 3

"Christopher, my friend! Over here!"

Chris turned in the direction of the voice and finally spotted Esteban, standing on the running board of a well-preserved antique automobile and waving enthusiastically over the heads of the milling crowd on the dock.

All around him there was controlled chaos. To Chris's left, a tour guide was attempting to marshal his restless charges while the ship's purser sorted through his collection of unclaimed suitcases for the luggage belonging to several of them. To the right, a young couple were being welcomed home by a huge and noisy family. In front and behind, passengers waiting to be met milled around at the foot of the gangplank. Chris had made a thorough search of the crowd. Nowhere could he see Colette Vaubois's lithe figure and engaging smile.

He'd been unable to locate her before the ship docked, even though he'd searched all of the likely places on board after finding her cabin already being

turned out by a steward. Then he'd stood at the top of
the gangplank as it was lowered, scanning the crowd
of disembarking passengers without seeing her. She
hadn't come down the gangplank after him, and the
ship was already being prepared for the return voyage. It was beginning to appear that she hadn't really
been aboard at all. That was impossible, he scolded
himself. He'd seen her name on the passenger list, for
heaven's sake! But how could he have missed her?

As Chris gazed hopefully around, pretending not to
be able to locate the source of Esteban's voice, his eyes
alighted momentarily on the heavily made-up face of
one of the young women on the guided tour. Her head
cocked, a small smile on her lips, she was studying
him, as her tangle of blond curls moved slightly in the
cool breeze. She had a dancer's figure and wore
snug-fitting blue jeans and a peasant blouse of coarse
cotton. This couldn't be Colette! The hair was the
wrong color . . . and yet there was a knowing arch to
her brows and a sort of tantalizing familiarity about
her face. . . .

Suddenly there was a warm hand on his arm and
Esteban was saying in a hearty voice, "Here I am,
Christopher. Can you ever forgive me for abandoning
you? What a crossing you must have had!"

As Chris turned, he put on a smile for his friend. "I
slept through most of it," he replied. "Besides, do you
think it would have been any calmer if you'd been
aboard?"

"It might have been. You never know," Esteban
declared with a wink.

Chris laughed. "Well, if the de Charracas can control the sea, then you ought to add 'below all' to your
family motto."

"I promise you I'll consider it," said Esteban, smiling. "Come—the taxi is waiting."

Chris glanced behind him once more, but the dock was nearly empty. The guide had marched his tour off to their hotel, the huge family had adjourned their celebration to a more private place, and most of the passengers had been met or were wandering off singly or in pairs. Chris heaved a regretful sigh.

"Is something wrong?" asked Esteban.

"Something I . . . wanted to do." Then, turning toward his friend Chris confessed, "I'm afraid I have bad news for you." It was the first time in hours that he'd thought about the art theft.

Esteban rubbed his chin thoughtfully. "I think I would prefer to hear it in my living room," he said, urging Chris toward the old car.

They drove in silence through a maze of white stucco boxes connected by clotheslines. Then the ancient taxicab passed through the triple gate leading out of Ibiza's old section and turned onto a narrow paved road. Moments later they were cruising between olive groves and fields of fragrant thyme as the cab headed toward the hill overlooking the bay of Ibiza.

"How was Paris when you left it?" Esteban asked suddenly.

Chris smiled ruefully. "Wet and cold."

Glancing at the by now rather rumpled denim suit Chris was wearing, Esteban remarked, "You really ought to get yourself a leather jacket while you're here. Leather goods are very reasonably priced in the Islands."

Chris nodded. "By the way," he said, "what was the emergency?"

"My ceiling was collapsing."

"What? In your house?" asked Chris, alarmed.

"No, no, at the dig. We've had a lot of rain this year," Esteban explained. "There was a leak, a water pocket formed, and the ceiling and walls of the excavation began to crack. Fortunately I arrived in time to shore up the roof—I'll show you later." Once Esteban had launched into his favorite subject, it scarcely mattered whether his audience was listening. Research was the count's only passion—he would give or do anything to continue his dig.

Feathery almond trees lined one side of the road, while some sheep grazed in a fenced field on the other side. Travel-weary, Chris leaned back in his seat and let Esteban's voice wash over him. He vaguely comprehended that the count was on the verge of a tremendous breakthrough, and he heard the name Carthage mentioned several times during the next ten miles.

"Forgive me," Esteban sighed at last. "I must be boring you with all this shoptalk."

"No," Chris assured him, stifling a yawn. "I'm just tired, that's all."

Esteban nodded his sympathy. At Santa Eulalia del Rio, a smaller and cleaner version of Ibiza, the taxi driver took a gravel road that spiraled upward to an unprepossessing-looking group of buildings perched on the hill. Halfway up the slope the cab pulled off the road and came to a halt in front of a painfully unadorned white stucco house shaped like an L. Climbing weeds had overgrown the low wall that surrounded the building and had all but woven a mat on the wrought-iron grills that protected the windows at the front of the house.

"Well," said the count with a heartiness that astounded Chris, "we're home."

CONTRARY TO CHRIS'S FIRST IMPRESSION of the house, Esteban hadn't forsaken *all* his creature comforts to be close to his dig. Cushioned by a marvelously overstuffed leather chair on one side of a brick fireplace in the living room, Chris sipped *palo* from a filigreed glass and wondered how he was going to break the news to his friend about the art theft.

"How do you like the liqueur?" Esteban asked, sinking into the chair facing his with an identical glass of dark brown liquid in his hand.

"It's good," Chris replied unenthusiastically.

"It's native to the Islands. We extract it from carob pods." Esteban raised his glass to his mouth, his dark eyes appraising his young friend as he sipped the bittersweet nectar. "All right, Christopher," he said, sighing as he put his drink down on the raised step in front of the hearth. "What's your bad news?"

"There was a theft in your house just before I left."

"Impossible!" Esteban declared. "Rosita or Hernan would have called me."

Chris stared miserably at the grate. "They might not know about it yet," he murmured brokenly. "It . . . happened in the museum, in the suite of rooms behind the dining room. All the paintings . . . ." His voice faded out and he shook his head sadly.

When Chris looked up again, he saw the count sitting bolt upright in his chair, his hands white-knuckled as they gripped the armrests. "How do you come to know about it?" Esteban asked tightly.

"I stumbled on the thieves while they were unframing the paintings."

"You saw them?"

"I saw the girl. The man came up behind me and...drugged me. When I woke up I was already aboard the ship."

Esteban was leaning forward in his seat, his face taut. "Describe the girl," he commanded in a soft voice.

A little puzzled, Chris complied. When he had finished, the count expelled his breath gustily and fell back against his chair, an ironic smile playing on his lips. "If you will excuse me, Christopher," Esteban said a few moments later, "I have a phone call to make."

"The police?"

Esteban shook his head, still smiling faintly.

"But you've been robbed!" Chris exclaimed indignantly. "Those paintings must have been worth a fortune!"

"I'm afraid you're wrong," the count said gently. "All the paintings in the *casa* are copies, worth no more than five or ten thousand *pesetas* each. Please excuse me." Esteban got up and disappeared into a room down the hall, leaving Chris's mind reeling.

Five thousand *pesetas* was about eighty dollars. And *all* the lovely oils and pastels he'd seen on the walls of the *casa* were copies? He remembered admiring one small painting, *The Adoration of the Magi* by Pablo Vergos, which hung in the main entrance hall. Enthralled by its delicacy, by the masterful technique of each brush stroke, Chris had reached out and, unable to bring himself to touch the canvas, had fingered instead the brass plaque bolted onto the bottom of the frame. Plunged into disillusionment by the count's regretful confession, Chris greeted him as he emerged from his office with the plaintive protest, "But not the Vergos!"

"I'm afraid even the Vergos is a copy," Esteban told him. "Christopher, you must have dreamed about a theft. I've just spoken to Hernan, and he swears on his mother's grave—a serious oath for him—that nothing is missing from the *casa*."

"If there were something missing," Chris pointed out slowly, "mightn't it reflect on his alertness . . . or his integrity?"

The count nodded thoughtfully and sat down. "Possibly," he conceded. "But I've known him and his family for years, and I don't think he's capable of lying to me, even over a long-distance phone line."

"You could always telephone the police—"

"No!" Seeming a little startled by the violence of his outburst, Esteban cleared his throat uncomfortably and explained in a gentler tone, "It mustn't become common knowledge that the de Charracas are . . . suffering financially. A police investigation would uncover the substitutions that have been made. I can't permit it."

Remembering the proud motto emblazoned over the portal of the *casa*, Chris could imagine just how painful such a disclosure would be for his friend. "Did you . . . sell them to finance your dig?" he asked.

"No." Esteban smiled ruefully. "I would have sold them, though. I was preparing to offer them privately when I had them appraised, in fact, and discovered that I'd been beaten to the punch by my brother, Diego."

"The one who, er, passed away about a year ago?" Chris spoke hesitantly, reluctant to stir up unpleasant memories.

Esteban nodded and took another sip of his *palo*. "You see, when our father died, he made no provision in his will for the estate to be divided, but simply willed it all to both of us. We continued to enjoy our separate life-styles, drawing money whenever we needed it and respecting—or so I thought—an informal agreement to leave the frozen assets untouched."

"But why wouldn't your father . . . ?"

Esteban smiled. "Because he was a de Charraca, and dividing up the estate would have meant admitting that he didn't trust his sons to act honorably toward each other. Family pride would never allow that."

Stunned at such lack of foresight, Chris merely stared at the count, who chuckled indulgently and explained, "Christopher, I realize this is hard for you to comprehend. The de Charraca family descends from a Catalan knight who led the reconquest of Ibiza during the fourteenth century. He was rewarded for his valor by being made a count and was then granted the north quarter of the island, with dominion over all the other Ibizan lords."

"That explains the motto," Chris murmured thoughtfully.

"It also explains my father's attitude. The de Charracas had to present a united front to the other landowners. It could never be revealed that we had as many internal squabbles as any other family, otherwise we might lose our stature on the island."

"That may have been true during the feudal era," Chris argued, "but surely in this day and age . . . ?"

Esteban shook his head. "This island lives in the past, Christopher. As each of the other noble families lost their wealth and their land, the de Charracas supposedly 'acquired' it. You may hear it said while you're here that I'm Ibiza's sole owner and could declare its independence if I chose."

"Is that true?"

"Theoretically, yes," Esteban admitted with a shrug, "although I have no legal claim to any land except for the three parcels whose deeds reside in my safe: the site of my dig, the half acre we're on right now and the ten acres around the old ruined castle on Charraca Bay." Esteban sighed wearily. "But I have no interest in politics," he added. "Not the way it's practiced nowadays. Diego used to tell me I was born two centuries too late. If so, Ibiza is the ideal place for me, for a while, anyway. When we go to mass later on you'll see why."

The two men sat sipping their liqueurs for several long moments before Chris finally worked up the nerve to ask, "When did the *casa* . . . ?"

"When did it become a museum?" his friend supplied in a voice surprisingly lacking in bitterness. "Shortly after Diego's death. When I learned that he'd sold all the paintings and hung copies in their place, I called in a gemologist to verify the authenticity of the Charraca family jewels." Esteban shrugged philosophically. "They turned out to be paste. The proceeds from the sale of the jewels alone would have paid the taxes and upkeep on the houses in Barcelona and Ibiza for fifteen years. The paintings would have funded my research for at least that long." He turned sad eyes on Chris's frowning face and continued, "So I had to sell the mansion in Ibiza and dispose of all the antiques on the second floor of the *casa*. I opened the first floor to the public, hoping that admission fees would cover the cost of maintaining the *casa*. If that plan fails, I'll just have to keep selling, one room after another."

Chris took a mouthful of *palo* but had difficulty swallowing it. "What could your brother have done with all that money?" he wondered aloud.

"I don't know," Esteban confessed wearily. "I found some receipts among his personal effects—various purchases, payments on a yacht that was later repossessed, and architects' and contractors' fees—but they don't account for one-tenth of what he must have realized from the sale of the jewels and paintings."

"Perhaps whatever the contractors were building for him—" Chris began, but Esteban cut him off with a disillusioned laugh.

"The contractors were playing along with one of Diego's quixotic fantasies. I never thought I would be admitting this to a . . . friend as new as you, Christopher, but my brother was an idealistic dreamer. He had a grandiose scheme for the reconstruction of the old castle on Charraca Bay. I've been out there, and he actually got as far as restoring the basement and the dungeon. What a foolish waste of time and money—but then Diego had never been solidly rooted in reality . . . ."

Chris carefully refrained from pointing out that Diego might have described his older brother's dig in equally harsh terms.

Just then the maid came in with coffee and two hearty sandwiches on a tray. "This is Soledad, Rosita's sister," Esteban said as she set the tray down on the raised hearth between the two men. After bobbing her head briefly in acknowledgment of her employer's introduction, Soledad turned and was gone with a swish of her long black skirt.

"Please help yourself," Esteban urged his guest, indicating the sandwiches made from thickly sliced, crusty white bread and generous portions of pungent red sausage and pickles. "The *sobrasada* comes from Soledad's *matanza*—that's an annual family festival that begins with the slaughter of the best pig the family owns and continues until everyone goes home with about a year's supply of pork products. Soledad's nephew puts some secret concoction of spices into his *sobrasada*, making it far superior to the types you'd buy in the market."

Taking enthusiastic bites of his sandwich, Chris could only agree.

As Esteban was pouring their second cup of coffee, Soledad reappeared to announce, "Miss Tirso is here to see you, sir."

"Send her right in," he replied without looking up. A pause, then, "Eva Tirso is my secretary. After a solid year of taking my dictation and transcribing my notes into legible form, she probably knows as much about ancient Carthage as I do."

"*Gracias,* Señor de Charraca," came a gentle voice from the doorway. "The extent of my knowledge also speaks of your ability as a teacher."

Esteban looked up with a strangely possessive smile and said, "Come in, Eva."

She was about twenty-five, Chris estimated, although he was learning that it was difficult to tell with Mediterranean women—their skin seemed to stay smoother longer than that of women in the north. Eva's dark hair was pulled back severely from her face and knotted at the nape of her neck, displaying a high forehead and finely drawn profile. She had delicately arched eyebrows and long thick lashes that would have been the envy of a professional model. In a country known for its striking women, Eva Tirso was pretty enough to hold her own.

Chris wasn't aware that he'd been staring at her until Esteban cleared his throat and commented significantly, "You'll be seeing a great deal of this young lady, Christopher. She'll be sitting at her typewriter in my office, just down the hall."

Smiling, Eva said a few polite words before excusing herself to go look for a book she'd left behind the previous day. As she turned, a whisper of taffeta made Chris realize how formally she was dressed, in a silver-trimmed blue dress with matching blue grogram cape. He mentioned this to Esteban, who explained that she was just on her way to mass.

"Ibizan women dress very plainly, except when they attend church. And at Eastertime you'll see even the youngest girls wearing taffeta and lace. In fact," Esteban added, consulting his watch, "it's nearly time *we* were setting off for mass. Perhaps you'd like to freshen up first. There's a chapel in Santa Eulalia, but I generally prefer the more impressive cathedral in Ibiza. However, Santa Eulalia is preparing a real spectacle for Good Friday—every year the townspeople stage a reenactment of the crucifixion."

Chris knew he should have objected. He was tired. He'd just arrived after more than twenty-four hours of travel and his luggage wasn't even unpacked. On top of that, he wasn't sure he'd brought anything suitable to wear to an impressive cathedral, and he knew better than to expect any stores to be open on Palm Sunday.

But he'd been raised to take the path of least resistance. Esteban was obviously a more devout Catholic than he was, or he would have thought twice about repeating the twelve-mile ride into Ibiza along unpaved roads. Esteban was also the host, and eleven years Chris's senior. It was a reflex reaction to agree with him. So, two hours later, Chris found himself standing at the Portal de las Tablas, the gate leading to the ancient walled city of Ibiza.

Families wearing their Sunday best stood admiring the window displays of darkened shops. Walking a pace or two behind their husbands, married women wore long silk dresses and shawls, while taffeta- or satin-clad girls paraded in groups of threes or fours, studiously ignoring the dark-suited young men they seemed so bent on impressing. Chris looked up and saw a sheep tethered to a balcony railing beside an old woman who was rocking and knitting, rocking and knitting with hypnotic rhythm.

"This gate is a fine example of old Roman statuary," declared Esteban beside him. Turning to look, Chris glimpsed something out of the corner of his eye that made his heart leap in his chest.

"Dolores!" he cried involuntarily.

Startled, the girl whirled around. She'd undergone a transformation since the last time he'd seen her. Now she was dressed in a long black skirt and matching tunic, and her hair hung in a single braid down her back, reaching almost to her waist. But she recognized him as completely as Chris had recognized her. With a shrill little gasp she turned and raced away from him down the street.

As Chris prepared to launch himself after her, a

large hand descended forcefully on his shoulder.

"Don't, Christopher," Esteban warned him tightly.

"But that's the girl . . . !" Chris began to protest.

"I know," said Esteban grimly. "Let her go."

Chapter 4

Esteban's house had been designed for a warm, sunny climate. Every wall was whitewashed, the floor was covered with bare tiles and the hallway leading to the guest room drew a constant flow of air from the patio on the other side of its wicker-trellised wall.

Chris was cold. He'd been given a room with a view of the coast, but a thick blanket of fog had rolled in, obscuring it. Furnished with only the bare necessities, the guest room was chilly and monkish and offered no distraction from the churning darkness of his thoughts.

Evidently, Esteban knew Dolores, and had known that she was one of the thieves from the first description Chris had given him. And yet the count had decided not to take legal action against her. Well, that was his privilege, Chris told himself—Esteban had assured him that none of the paintings was worth much. But it jarred with what Chris knew of the de Charraca code of ethics to let a criminal or even an attempted criminal get off that easily, no matter how petty the theft.

Something wasn't adding up right. True, there were limits to how much you could learn about a person in the space of eight months' acquaintance. Chris had thought the gaps in his knowledge about his friend were normal and nothing to be concerned about—until now. Suddenly it was of paramount importance to discover who Dolores was and what her connection was to Count Esteban de Charraca.

In a moment of overriding decisiveness Chris strode into the living room where Esteban sat reading a magazine. There would be time for deviousness later if the direct approach failed.

"Esteban, I have something to ask you."

Slowly the count put down his historical journal. "Oh?" he murmured.

Taking a deep breath, Chris blurted out, "I have to know about Dolores. Why didn't you let me go after her this afternoon?"

"What would you have done if you'd caught up with her?" Esteban countered.

Chris opened his mouth to answer, but the count cut him off with a gesture. "Dolores is a child of the slums," he said. "Five or six generations ago her family and the de Charracas were on equal footing. Now her father lives in a hovel in the fishermen's quarter of Ibiza."

"And out of generosity you've decided not to prosecute?" demanded Chris, amazed.

"There's nothing to prosecute, my friend," Esteban replied with a shrug. "Nothing was taken."

"You have only your gatekeeper's word on that."

"Hernan would not lie to me," Esteban insisted stubbornly.

"All right then, assuming Hernan was telling the

truth and nothing turned up missing, I still witnessed an attempt, Esteban!" Chris couldn't keep his puzzlement and anger out of his voice.

Esteban frowned impatiently. Then he said, in a voice that held an unspoken warning, "There are good reasons for my decision, Christopher, and until such time as I choose to share them with you, you'll just have to trust me."

"I see," said Chris, realizing that his friend couldn't be pushed any further. "Forgive me for being indiscreet."

"You were just voicing your concern," the count replied stiffly. "I quite understand." But the scowl on his face said something entirely different.

The following morning Esteban greeted Chris cheerfully at breakfast, as though their discussion of the night before had never taken place. Buttering a sweet roll, Esteban asked, "Well, Christopher, are you ready to visit my dig?"

"Of course," Chris replied casually. "Are we packing a lunch?"

Esteban took a hasty sip of his coffee. "That isn't necessary. The site is only three and a half miles from here. But there's quite a cutting wind outside. You'll need a sweater." He stood up. "Wait here a moment," he said and disappeared down the corridor. A minute later he was back, wearing a thick brown turtleneck sweater and carrying a green one over his arm. "Why don't you put this on?" he suggested, and Chris accepted the warm garment gratefully.

They stepped outside into the driving wind. Just then a canopied mule-drawn cart pulled up at the door, driven by a short, sinewy man with a thick black mustache that made him look like a Mexican *bandito*.

He wore a battered black felt hat securely fastened beneath his chin by straps, and loose-fitting denim coveralls. As he stopped the cart he tipped his hat ceremoniously to the men standing in the doorway. *"Buenos días, señores,"* he said.

"Good morning, Jondalitx," Esteban replied briskly, waving Chris into the cart and climbing in after him. "Jondalitx is my foreman, Christopher. He's also Soledad's nephew, the one who makes such delicious *sobrasada*."

Jondalitx smiled briefly over his shoulder, then turned his full attention to his driving, leaving Esteban to explain that the road to the dig was narrow and treacherous, and even a mule cart could run into problems if the driver were careless.

As they topped a gentle rise, a dark ravine suddenly appeared on their right, paralleling the road for several hundred yards before veering off to join a distant creekbed. Just then Esteban nudged Chris and said proudly, "Look over there. That stone bridge was built by the Romans more than two thousand years ago and it's still solid. We can come back for a closer look when the weather clears."

Before Chris could make any kind of response the cart turned abruptly onto a bumpy trail that traced the foot of a lofty, fog-shrouded ridge. This was Puig Fita, which Esteban was convinced held the key to so many mysteries of Ibiza's past. Now they were following the edge of a cliff, rounding the back of the ridge as below them a wind-whipped sea lathered itself against the sharp rocks.

The entrance to the site looked like an abandoned mining operation. Chris saw a squat doorway framed by rain-warped boards, and a tunnel entrance so uniformly black that it seemed painted onto the side of the ridge. Jondalitx stopped the cart and got down, handing the reins over to Esteban before going to join the other workers.

"There's a sheltered place farther along where the mule can stand. Even on good days the wind can be a problem here," Esteban explained, urging the animal forward another hundred feet. From this new vantage point Chris was able to look out over the long deep bay of Cala Llonga. Today it was blue gray, reflecting the stormy sky overhead. Twenty yards below them, on a protected strip of beach, a small donkey was struggling to pull a cartload of stones through the yielding sand.

This dig *could* have been a primitive attempt to mine the ridge—or the setting for a horror movie, Chris mused wryly as he followed Esteban along a narrow passageway lit by acetylene lamps. Hung from pegs, which had been pounded into the wall of the tunnel, the lanterns cast a flurry of multiple shadows, heightening the eerie impression that They Were Not Alone.

Suddenly Esteban reached up and plucked a lamp off its peg, then disappeared into a gash in the rock wall. Chris hesitated for a moment at the opening, noticing in the afterglow of his friend's lantern that the sides of the narrow tunnel had been hastily shored up with timbers of various sizes. This must be the part of the dig that had threatened to collapse earlier.

Determinedly squelching his uncertainty about the safety of the tunnel, Chris followed Esteban into the slitlike opening; but he hadn't taken more than six or seven cautious steps before the tunnel ended at a rough stone wall. Gazing around in disappointment,

Chris said in a half whisper, "But there's nothing here."

"Not yet, but soon," replied Esteban, proudly patting the wall. "Take a close look at this—I think it was constructed during the Carthaginian occupation. Cala Llonga would have been an important military harbor then, and I'm betting that we've discovered the foundation of a fourth- or fifth-century B.C. Carthaginian fortress."

Slowly Chris reached out and touched the rough-hewn stones. While still an undergraduate he'd traveled through most of Europe, visiting scores of ancient monuments, in an attempt to capture the flavor of European history. Awed by its majesty, he'd touched one of the towering monoliths of Stonehenge and found to his disappointment that it felt like any other rock. He still wasn't sure what he'd been expecting—the fragile dryness usually associated with old age, perhaps, or the hollow delicacy of a vacated sea-snail shell—but he'd left England feeling somehow cheated. Only later had he come to realize that many of the stones on earth were equally ancient, the only difference between them being what various men had chosen to make with them. The true wonder of Stonehenge was that human beings had set it in place, marking a primitive achievement that it was suggested only a space-age technology could duplicate. And the wonder of this ancient fortress lay in the fact that human energy and skill had gone into its construction, and that human lives had been spent defending it, almost twenty-five hundred years ago. The bones of those Carthaginian soldiers had long since fallen into dust, but the stone in the fortress remained.

"Let's go back outside and let the workmen do their

job," Esteban suggested quietly. Wordlessly Chris followed him toward the daylight.

CHRIS'S STOMACH CHURNED as he stared at his lunch plate of cold meat and spicy vegetable salad. Almost twenty-four hours had passed since he'd spotted Dolores near the Roman gate in Ibiza, a full day gone and not one of the nagging questions in his mind even close to being answered. Chris could feel his tension growing, tying him up in knots. He had to do something!

"Esteban," he began, pausing a little uncertainly as both Eva and the count looked up at him. "I'm afraid I won't be able to return with you to the dig this afternoon. I have to go into Ibiza."

"Naturally, you're free to go where you wish, Christopher," his host assured him. "You're here on a vacation, after all."

"Yes, of course," Chris agreed, but his voice lacked conviction. Esteban had carefully refrained from asking his reason for going into town, and Chris wondered if he was thinking about their discussion of the previous day and drawing the obvious conclusion.

It was a breach of hospitality to continue prying into a matter that Esteban had explicitly told him to drop, but Esteban wasn't the only one it affected. Chris had been assaulted and drugged by the intruders he'd surprised in the *casa*, and then they'd forwarded him like stray luggage to the island. He didn't trust their motives for setting him loose—if indeed that was what they'd done—and he had no guarantee that they wouldn't set upon him again, at a time and place better suited to their purpose. The best way to avoid that was to get some straight answers to his questions, and the likeliest person to ask was the thief whose father now lived in a hovel in the fishermen's quarter of Ibiza.

"What's the best way to get into town?" Chris asked casually.

Esteban consulted his watch. "If you hurry you can catch the two o'clock bus," he replied. "But it's always so crowded. . . . Why don't you take my bicycle?"

"It's a twelve-mile ride," Chris reminded him. "Perhaps if the weather were more pleasant. . . ."

"Shall I call Mr. Laval a taxi, *señor*?" This was the first time Eva had spoken since they'd sat down to eat. Chris expected Esteban to be displeased with her for undermining his obvious efforts to discourage Chris from going into Ibiza, but the count merely smiled and nodded his approval.

"That's an excellent idea, Eva," Esteban murmured.

Blushing fiercely, she excused herself to make the phone call, disappearing before Chris could thank her.

CHRIS GOT OUT OF THE TAXI in a rundown neighborhood some distance past the Roman gates. Here, on the outer margins of the gracious, aristocratic older section of town, the narrow streets were twisting and uneven. Chris saw rows of closely set houses, yellowed with age and all showing signs of neglect. The dwellings became more primitive as he strolled, until they were little more than squat white boxes barely six feet high, interconnected by a haphazard network of clotheslines where flapping fishing nets and patched clothing seemed to jockey for drying space.

It was a slum, and yet there was nothing sinister or unhealthy about it, despite its abject poverty. Small children frolicked noisily in the narrow streets, loosely supervised by the housewives who stood calling to each other from their respective doorways. There was none of the filth here that was often left to accumulate in the back streets of some Mediterranean cities. There weren't even any beggars.

Chris stopped to ask one of the housewives whether she knew of any impoverished noblemen, with a daughter named Dolores, living in the district. The woman only shrugged, but a younger version of herself, wearing the same long black skirt and black bandanna over her hair, called from a doorway across the street, "Maybe he means old Antonio."

Immediately the first woman retorted sharply, "Antonio has no daughter!"

Unperturbed, the younger woman replied, "But he had one once."

"Well, he doesn't anymore!" And the first woman went into her house and slammed the door.

His curiosity piqued, Chris strode across the street. "Why doesn't he have a daughter anymore?" he inquired politely.

"Because he disowned her."

"Do you know why?"

She shrugged philosophically. "Nobody knows why," she told him. "He just did." And now it was her turn to go inside and close the door in his face.

For several moments Chris stood in the middle of the unpaved street, a little nonplussed by this latest development. If the Dolores he sought was old Antonio's disowned daughter, the odds were against the old man's even wanting to talk about her with a stranger, let alone give him her address. Still, this was the only lead he had. With a sigh, Chris turned to ask another of the housewives for directions to old Antonio's house, and at that instant he glimpsed a

slender, black-clad female form ducking hastily into
an alleyway. Smiling grimly, he hurried after her.
What a stroke of luck to run across Dolores again!

Chris could easily have caught up with her and
forced a confrontation then and there, but he'd already decided that such a move would be foolish. This
island was Dolores's home, while he was a foreigner
here. Disowned or not, she was far likelier than Chris
was to get the benefit of the doubt if any of her
countrymen became involved in any dispute he had
with her. Chris had already been made painfully
aware of how little evidence he possessed that the girl
was a thief; all she had to do was yell for help and he
could well wind up behind bars. So he followed her at
a discreet distance, hoping she'd lead him to her home
where he could talk to her. Dolores seemed remark-
ably oblivious to his presence. Chris had assumed that
she'd fled down the twisting laneway because she had
seen him standing in the street, and yet she never even
looked over her shoulder. Instead, walking at a brisk
pace she led him down to the sea.

The fishermen's port wasn't as aesthetically pleas-
ing as the tourists' marina. Near the long wooden
platforms where the catch was cleaned before being
packed in ice for shipping, there was a pervasive
aroma that not even the stiff breeze from the sea could
banish. Everywhere Chris looked he saw scrawny
cats: some were fighting over fish heads, while others
perched sentinel-like on barrels or dozed peacefully in
doorways as they waited for the boats to return.
Meanwhile, across the slate-gray water of the harbor,
the ruins of an ancient fortress wall slashed at the sky
like the jagged bottom of a broken bottle.

At the very moment Chris glanced at this remnant

of the past he tripped over a half-buried stone and crashed to the ground painfully. When he picked himself up Dolores was no longer in sight. He stopped and stared forlornly around, but she had vanished into the maze of twisting alleyways, where Chris knew he could search for hours without finding her. *Damn!*

Suddenly a man stepped out from behind some crates that were stacked on the pier. Thickset and fortyish, he wore a blue T-shirt and worn gray trousers. As he pitched his cigarette butt into the water and turned toward Chris, a momentary frown crossed his face before he turned his back to the young man once more. Even though the man had grown a mustache since the last time they'd spoken, Chris recognized him at once. He was the father of one of Chris's students, and the last person Chris expected to find on Ibiza.

"Captain Hurteau! How are you?" Chris called out in French. "I never expected to run into you here." Smiling, Chris approached with one hand extended to shake the captain's, but the other man kept both his hands at his sides and turned to gaze blankly at him.

"Perdóne me," he muttered. *"Yo no comprendo."*

Stunned, Chris stammered in Spanish, "Oh. I'm sorry, sir. You . . . you look just like someone I know."

The man nodded and returned to his contemplation of the bay as Chris, after a moment's hesitation, began the trek back to the taxi stand near the Roman gates. He could have sworn that that man was Lucien Hurteau's father, a retired army officer. They'd talked often and long about Canada a couple of months ago. When Chris had mentioned that he'd be going home for a visit during the upcoming summer, the captain had suggested that he look up some of Hurteau's cousins who lived near Chris's hometown. Surely Hurteau couldn't have forgotten that! Chris shook his head. The Hurteau he'd talked to was an expensively dressed government official of some sort, not this scruffy-looking Spaniard. He *must* have made a mistake.

Chris was passing the entrance to an alleyway even narrower than the one he was in, when his thoughts were disrupted by a persistent hissing sound. Puzzled, he stopped and looked around. And then a hand reached out of the shadows and yanked him brutally into the alley.

This was it, he thought wildly. The thieves had found him alone in a deserted spot and were going to silence him for good. As he struggled desperately Chris suddenly felt something hard pressing against his ribs. A gravelly voice whispered in French into his ear, "Freeze or I'll shoot."

Chris froze.

"Laval," his attacker hissed, "what the hell are you doing here?"

For the first time Chris took a good look at his attacker. It was the stranger he'd mistaken for Hurteau . . . only it *was* Hurteau! "Captain?" he ventured.

"You didn't answer my question." The captain's voice was cold.

For a moment Chris thought the man was joking. But only for a moment. The hand that held the gun stuck in his side was steady, and the eyes that surveyed him were almost clinical in their detachment. *Almost as if I've ceased to exist as a person*, Chris thought, a shiver going through him.

"I . . . I'm staying with Count Esteban de Charraca,"

Chris's voice came out in a croak. "I'm his guest. He's working on—"

"Never mind that. I know all about the count. What I want to know is, who told you I'd be here?"

Chris's boyish looks emphasized the expression of surprise on his face. "W-what? Nobody! I mean, why should I want to know where you are? Look, Captain Hurteau, what the hell's going on?"

The captain stared at Chris for a moment, then, as if coming to some decision, he nodded and pocketed his gun. "Okay. So it's a coincidence. But it could be a costly one for me. I can't be sure your little salutation at the top of your lungs didn't blow my cover. And the name is Roig; Fernando Roig."

Chris's mind, released from the grip of fear that had all but petrified it a few minutes before, was now ticking over like well-oiled machinery. "Am I to take it then that you work for the government in an, er, unorthodox capacity?"

The captain scowled. "And what if I did?"

Chris flushed. "Then I'm sorry if I loused it up for you. I wish there were some way I could make up for my blunder," he said, sensing as he spoke them how lame the words were. To his surprise, however, Hurteau/Roig rubbed his chin thoughtfully.

"Perhaps you *can* help, Laval," he said slowly. "Let me get back to you."

"How will you contact me?" Chris queried.

Hurteau shrugged. "Don't worry about it. You're not hard to keep tabs on."

Suddenly something clicked in Chris's mind and he blurted out, "Was that you following me in Barcelona?"

"No," Hurteau replied carefully. "You were fol-

lowed, eh? Tell me about it." When Chris had finished
the captain smiled grimly. "Well, well. Now isn't that
interesting. Yes, I think I can definitely say you'll be
able to help us, Laval. Just go about your business. I'll
be in touch." And with that he melted into the
shadows and disappeared.

Chapter 5

Esteban was sitting in one of the easy chairs in the living room, feigning interest in a dog-eared magazine when Chris returned to the house late that afternoon.

"I wasn't expecting you back so early," the count murmured. He flipped the remaining pages idly and dropped the journal back into its wire rack.

Chris shrugged uncomfortably and sank down in the opposite chair. "It isn't that far to Ibiza by cab," he remarked.

Leaning back in his seat, Esteban gazed fixedly into Chris's face. "Well, did you find her?" he muttered.

Chris decided there was no use beating around the bush. "Yes, I did," he replied, "but she got away before I could talk to her. You could save me a great deal of trouble, you know, by simply telling me who she is."

"She's nobody."

"Her name is Dolores," Chris challenged him. "And I suspect she might be Antonio's daughter, the one he disowned."

"Who told you that?" Esteban sounded suddenly tired.

"Is it true?"

"Yes."

After a thoughtful pause, Chris asked, "Did his reason for disowning her have anything to do with her . . . life of crime?"

Esteban raised both hands, then let them fall to the arms of his chair in a gesture of helpless ignorance. "Possibly," he conceded.

"I'm only trying to understand why you refuse to take legal action against her," Chris explained earnestly. "Several possibilities come to mind, but I'm afraid they aren't very flattering to you, Esteban."

The count smiled thinly. "I thought we knew each other better than that," he chided.

Feeling vaguely ashamed, Chris replied, "I'm beginning to realize that I hardly know you at all."

"Perhaps that's true," Esteban sighed. "I keep forgetting that nearly eleven years separate us. And in terms of morals and ethics, the gap is probably much wider than that." As Chris drew himself up to protest this apparent slur on his character, the count went on, "Diego was right—I should have been born two hundred years ago, when a man's duty was more strictly defined than it is now. . . . "

"Is there really that much difference?"

Esteban snorted derisively. "There is a world of difference," he declared. "Even on my old-fashioned Ibiza, everything is turning upside down. We've been discovered, Christopher—by pleasure-seeking tourists, by tax-evading immigrants, by profit-hungry developers. It's a no less catastrophic invasion than any military landing in Ibiza's past, because of the traumatic changes it's wreaking in our peaceful way of life. The very fabric of our society is being threatened."

As Chris leaned back skeptically in his chair, Esteban went on, "For example, Ibizan farmers traditionally pass their finest land on to their most favored heirs and their least arable property to the black sheep of the family. They've been doing that for hundreds of generations." Chris nodded. "Along come the developers wanting to put up villas and condominiums, and suddenly the most valuable land on the island turns out to be in the hands of all the ne'er-do-wells— the dry, rocky soil along the coast is now worth enough to guarantee a life of luxury in Barcelona while the rest of the family go on breaking their backs back home on the farm!" he concluded indignantly.

Refusing to be distracted, Chris said quietly, "Do you know why Dolores was disowned?"

Esteban sighed. "You're very persistent, Christopher. Does it really mean that much to you to know?"

Nodding gravely, Chris replied, "Now more than ever, I'm afraid."

"And once your curiosity is satisfied . . . ?"

"It'll go no further, I promise you."

Esteban exhaled gustily and squeezed his eyes shut for a moment. Then, apparently resigned to this invasion of his privacy, he murmured, "Very well, then. Dolores's full name is Dolores Anguila de Charraca. She's Diego's widow."

Chris uttered a low whistle. "That explains a great deal," he said softly. "But she wasn't disowned . . . ?

"For marrying my brother? No," Esteban replied sadly. "She did something . . . afterward . . . that brought dishonor to both our families. And that's all I'm going to say about it."

"I understand," Chris said respectfully. "Thank you for what you did tell me, Esteban."

When Chris left the living room, the count was slumped in his chair, scowling at the fireplace.

CHRIS ARRIVED FOR BREAKFAST the following morning filled with uncertainty. Esteban had been "indisposed" the previous evening, leaving Chris to dine alone, and judging from the daggerlike looks Soledad had shot him as she brought him his meal, the housekeeper obviously blamed Chris for upsetting her employer. Dinner had been an unpleasant affair. The food had not sat well on his stomach, and Chris dreaded a repetition of the ordeal at breakfast.

But Esteban was halfway through his omelet when Chris appeared at the table, and he only glanced up briefly as the younger man sat down.

"What's this?" Chris muttered, picking up the envelope that had been placed under his fork.

"It arrived this morning for you, hand delivered," Soledad told him as she leaned over to pour his coffee. The casual indifference in her voice told Chris that he'd been forgiven for yesterday, and the neutral curiosity in Esteban's eyes when they met Chris's across the table was a further reassurance.

"You may as well open it," Soledad prodded him. "Your breakfast won't be ready for another few minutes."

Chris tore open the envelope. There was a single sheet of paper inside, bearing a cryptic message: "Ten o'clock this morning, by the sailors' monument, Ibiza waterfront. Roig."

"Well, Christopher," said Esteban heartily, dabbing

at his mouth with his napkin, "will you be joining me at the dig this morning?"

"I'm . . . afraid not, Esteban," Chris apologized. This would have to be handled delicately. He could already feel his mouth going dry. "I've been asked to meet someone in town."

The count frowned reprovingly. "Is it Dolores?" he inquired.

Chris shook his head. "This is . . . someone else," he replied evasively. "Someone I met for the first time yesterday."

With a knowing nod, Esteban said, "I see. . . . You're still welcome to borrow my bicycle."

"Thanks for the offer, but I think I'd rather take a cab," Chris replied apologetically.

Esteban shrugged. "As you wish, my friend. But you'll have to make the phone call yourself when you're ready, since Eva is going to be late this morning. I believe she has the number written down in the address book on her desk."

"That's fine," Chris assured him as the count got up and headed toward the tiny vestibule. "Have a good day."

Esteban threw him an impenetrable look just before disappearing through the door.

Chris tried to do justice to Soledad's steaming omelet smothered in fragrant tomato sauce, but the message from Captain Hurteau lying beside his coffee cup was a constant reminder of the sinister world Chris had inadvertently stumbled into the previous day, and his appetite deserted him. Thanks to his own stupidity, that shady realm of espionage was reaching out to Chris like a many-tentacled monster. He could feel his stomach sinking with the realization that it would ensnare him, one way or another. For a moment he was seized with the desire to run, to get away as quickly as he could. But the impulse was quashed. How could he ignore a summons from a representative of the French government?

"I think I'll make that phone call now," Chris muttered and got up from the table. Soledad's face twisted with exasperation as she removed his barely touched breakfast.

There were two desks in Esteban's office. One was cluttered with stacks of files and pages of scribbled notes. The other was tidy and orderly, with neat stacks of bond typing paper on a retractable shelf beside the sleek modern electric typewriter, and a matched set of containers for paper clips, pencils and memo slips. On the floor beside this second desk, which was obviously Eva's, sat a black leather notebook with the word "addresses" stamped in gold on the cover. But it also contained phone numbers, as Chris saw when he picked it up and opened it to the first page.

The entries were arranged alphabetically. Chris turned to T for taxi, but the page was empty. He shook his head in vexation. What had been the name on the side of that old car? Aragones? Gonsalves? There was a "gon" in it somewhere....

He turned to the G's and scanned the list quickly: Garapina, Gacetillero, Galgo, Gancho, Ganzúa, Gomez—

"What are you doing?" Eva's voice was hard with fury. Startled, Chris looked up and found her glaring at him from the doorway, her dark eyes flashing with barely controlled rage as her fists clenched and unclenched at her sides.

He smiled his apology. "I wanted to call a taxi, and—"

"Where did you get that?" she demanded tightly.

Bewildered, Chris closed the book. "It was on the floor," he explained uncertainly. "Esteban told me you had the number written down and I just assumed when I saw it lying there that it had dropped off your desk. I'm sorry," he concluded lamely.

"You should have asked me," she said, her voice a little softer.

"You weren't expected in until much later this morning, and I have to be in Ibiza by ten."

Eva's eyes opened wide with surprise. "Who told you I'd be late?" she blurted out.

"Esteban."

After an uncomfortable pause lasting several seconds, Eva approached him and said, "I'll call your taxi, Mr. Laval. That's my private address book," she explained, taking it from him and slipping it into her purse. "It must have fallen out of my purse by accident."

"I'm sorry, I didn't know."

She shrugged briefly. "No harm done." Lifting up the container of memo slips, Eva uncovered another, much smaller address book, and while she was flipping through it Chris walked out of the office.

Half an hour later his taxi arrived, and as he stepped through the front door, he read the name Segonales on the side of the cab. These Ibizans had such strange names, he reflected as the driver negotiated the bumpy road at breakneck speed. Segonales sounded like Seconal, the trade name of a sedative. And the names in Eva's address book had been equally unusual—Garapina was a sort of candy, Galgo was Spanish

for greyhound and Ganzúa translated as skeleton key.
He couldn't recall the others. . .

The sailors' monument was located near the
tourists' marina. As he stepped out of the taxi, Chris
noticed that the docks were empty. However, at the
foot of the monument—a gravestone-shaped slab
dedicated to all the Ibizans who had been lost at
sea—he recognized the tall, slender woman gazing
out over the bay.

Chris gulped hard. She was the last person he
expected to find here. Where was Roig? As he strode
toward Dolores, the Mediterranean sun burst through
an opening in the clouds, deepening the blue of the
bay and making the city seem to glow around them.

"Hello, Dolores," he said softly. "I wasn't expecting
to see you today."

"Life is full of surprises, Señor Laval." Her voice
was a gentle soprano with a natural trill to it that Chris
found very pleasant. He noticed that she was still
wearing her black skirt and tunic.

She cleared her throat. "Are you ready to see Roig?"
she asked.

"If he's ready to see me," Chris replied with feigned
confidence. Bewildered by the turn of events, he still
felt as though he was walking into a trap. He couldn't
be sure that the note he'd received came from Roig.

Dolores turned and pointed to the end of one of the
jetties in the marina. "There's a rowboat tied to the
end of that pier. It's been rented in your name for the
next hour. Row out to the launch that's anchored in
the middle of the bay and wait for further instructions."

"Is Roig out there?" Chris asked, but Dolores just
shrugged. As he turned to walk toward the jetty she

moved off, and by the time he had reached the boat, she was nowhere to be seen.

"Curiouser and curiouser," he muttered to himself as he stepped carefully into the flimsy-looking dinghy. What was a Spanish art thief doing working with French Intelligence?

Ten minutes later, the rowboat was alongside the blue and white launch that bobbed beside the marker buoy in the channel. "Ahoy there!" Chris called out as he shipped the oars, straining to discern any signs of life aboard the larger craft. It was, strictly speaking, not a launch at all, but rather a stripped-down forty-foot cruiser that had seen better days.

"Come aboard, Mr. Laval," Roig's voice floated down to him.

Chris tied his dinghy to the ladder hanging over the side of the cruiser and climbed up. As he sat opposite Roig on the deck, the agent asked, "Well, Mr. Laval, are you still willing to help us out?"

"Of course," Chris replied, more confidently than he felt.

"That's good. Because you now know just enough to jeopardize this mission. If you'd said no we would have had to remove you."

"Remove me?" Chris echoed faintly.

"Only temporarily, of course, until the mission was over. You would have been inconvenienced—" Suddenly Roig burst out laughing. "Good grief, man, what did you think I meant? We don't go around cold-bloodedly murdering every innocent bystander who blunders into our path, you know!"

Secretly relieved, Chris smiled wanly.

Roig handed him a photograph, which he'd pulled out of a canvas fishing-tackle bag behind him. "That's

the man who's been following you. His name is
Bertoldo. And he's an agent we've been after for some
time."

Bertoldo had blond hair and Teutonic features. A
scar ran halfway down his left cheek, and Chris
noticed that the photo looked as grim and posed as a
passport picture . . . or a mug shot.

"I want you to commit his face to memory," Roig
continued. "You're going to help us trap him."

"Trap him?" Startled, Chris glanced up and met
Roig's stern gray eyes.

The agent sighed. "We've cut the risk to a minimum
for you, Laval, so don't worry. We already know he's
somewhere on the island. He's probably still keeping
tabs on you, somehow. All we want you to do for the
time being is circulate, do all the things that tourists do
on Ibiza. You'll be a kind of bait for us."

"That sounds simple enough," Chris conceded,
though he didn't like the word "bait." "Why is he
following me anyway?"

The agent shrugged. "When we catch him we'll find
that out. In the meantime if you happen to spot him
send word to me through Jondalitx, the foreman at the
count's dig. Then sit tight and wait for further instructions." Chris's expression must have been eloquent,
for Roig reminded him wryly, "The mission isn't over
until Bertoldo is out of circulation. I thought you
wanted to help?"

"It isn't that, it's only. . . ." Chris licked his lips and
took a deep breath before asking, "Is Count de Charraca involved in this?"

Roig frowned. "No, he isn't, and if you let on to him
that you're working with me he won't give you a
moment's peace. He knows me from a previous as-

signment, in which I had to make him hate me in order to get closer to certain other people. Now he thinks I'm a blackhearted scoundrel, and that's a shame, because I'd like to know him better. However, those are the breaks of the game." Roig sighed. "Any other questions?"

Ignoring Roig's sarcasm, Chris replied, "Yes. What's this all about? Why is Bertoldo so important to you?"

The agent seemed taken aback by his temerity. After a pause Roig said, "You don't really want an answer to that, do you? You already know more than is good for your health." He paused. "Now, do you understand what you're supposed to do?"

"Yes."

"All right. Return the dinghy to the foot of the pier and go about your business. And just remember this—if you do as you're told you'll be okay. Don't try any heroics on your own. You may not get a second chance."

Chapter 6

Good Lord, what have I got myself into now?

Chris fidgeted restlessly in the backseat of the taxicab as the full horror of his situation was borne in on him. He'd committed himself to what amounted to a conspiracy to kidnap, perhaps even kill, another man. And now that he'd placed himself under Roig's command he could find himself being ordered to do just about anything, including taking an active part in the business. What could have possessed him to make him agree to such a scheme? Chris wasn't secret-agent material and knew it.

I should have refused and let him "remove" me. Or better yet, I should have refused and then run like hell to Canada . . . . This whole thing was getting out of control.

Nonetheless, by the time the taxi pulled up in front of Esteban's house, Chris had not only resigned himself to making the best of a bad situation, he'd even come up with a story to tell the count that would cover up his connections with Fernando Roig. Rehearsing it in his head, Chris paid the cab fare and stepped into the house.

Almost instantly Soledad appeared in the kitchen doorway with her hands on her ample hips. "Back already?" she sniffed. "I hope you're not hungry, because the count is still out and lunch won't be ready for another hour."

"That's all right," Chris replied, a little disappointed at having to wait to tell his carefully prepared lie. The housekeeper nodded and vanished again.

Just then the rhythmic clicking of Eva's typewriter, which had formed the background to this exchange, suddenly faltered and stopped. Seconds later Eva emerged from the office holding a thick manila envelope in her hand. "I'm going down to the post office in Santa Eulalia now," she called into the kitchen. "Do you want anything picked up?"

Soledad grumbled something unintelligible.

As Eva passed him in the hall, Chris remarked, "It's a long walk into town."

"It's only twenty minutes there and back by bicycle," she rejoined. "Excuse me, *señor*."

It wasn't until she was pedaling out of sight that Chris realized there hadn't been an address on the envelope.

"WELL, CHRISTOPHER, did this . . . other person put in an appearance?" Esteban's question sounded casual, but Chris could sense the tension behind the words. Taking a deep breath, he launched into his cover story.

"Yes, she did," he replied with a smile.

"She?" The count paused in the act of reaching for the olive tray. "Is this another tourist?"

"Er, no. She made me promise not to tell her name

because she doesn't want to jeopardize her reputation. It's an Ibizan girl I met on the boat from Barcelona."

Esteban smiled. "I wondered who you were looking for on the dock," he said indulgently, shaking his head.

"So it's possible that she'll be sending me more notes and that I'll have to slip away to meet her at odd hours . . . you understand," Chris went on. Suddenly he had the sensation of eyes boring into the side of his head. He turned and caught Eva staring intently at him, an instant before she lowered her gaze modestly to her plate of salad.

"Are you serious about this girl, Christopher?" Esteban asked with a frown. "Because if you are, then perhaps you should declare your intentions openly at her *festeig*, instead of sneaking off to secret meetings."

"*Festeig*? That sounds like a mangled version of *festejo*," Chris remarked.

"It is. Social practices are very formalized on Ibiza, and that includes courtship. A *festeig* is a wooing. The young lady stands at the door to her house and gives each of her suitors a chance to court her while she remains absolutely silent. This goes on as long as she wishes, and any man may woo her. When she chooses, her decision is final." Chris thought he detected a note of sadness in Esteban's voice at the end of the explanation.

"I've only known her for three days, Esteban," he said uncomfortably. "I doubt that either of us is ready for final decisions at this point."

"Of course not," the count sighed. "You're right. But be aware that you're taking a tremendous risk, not just with her reputation but also with your safety. If she's had a traditional upbringing, her family would frown quite heavily on passing flirtations with foreign tourists."

"You mean her brothers might come after me?" Chris smiled crookedly.

"That's crudely put but probably accurate," Esteban replied. "And you'd have no legal redress."

Terrific! Chris thought wryly. His story seemed to have covered absolutely every angle, even providing an explanation in the event that his body was fished out of the bay.

After Esteban had returned to the dig that afternoon, Chris decided to borrow a bicycle and tour Santa Eulalia. The sky had cleared and, according to the weather reports, would remain blue and sunny the rest of the week.

Santa Eulalia could be called a town only by virtue of the fact that it possessed a bus station. That it also had a post office, a grocery store and a movie house was irrelevant as far as Chris was concerned: what elevated it from villagehood was its transportation link with Ibiza.

Chris's initial impression of Santa Eulalia had been influenced by the hasty glimpses of Ibiza, which he'd caught through the windows of Esteban's taxicab that first morning. But he'd since had the opportunity to explore sections of the larger city, and now that he was seeing the small town up close Chris realized that there was very little similarity between the two places. Ibiza had the gracious older quarter and the busy commercial areas to balance off the slums on its outskirts—Santa Eulalia had nothing. It could still have been a successful resort, like the many villages on the Riviera, if its poverty weren't so much in evi-

dence—and if the "beach" were something more than
an abbreviated stretch of shoreline strewn with sharp
rocks.

On his way up the beach path, Chris decided to stop
in at the post office and satisfy his curiosity on a point
that had been nagging at him since before lunch. The
clerk behind the badly marred oak counter was young,
with the same shy, deferential manner Chris had
noticed Eva Tirso using with Esteban.

"Good afternoon," Chris said, in what he hoped
was a brisk, businesslike voice. "Has Señorita Tirso
been in today?"

The clerk shook his head thoughtfully. "No, *señor*.
Was she supposed to come in?"

"I gave her something to mail for me and I was just
curious to know whether it had got off."

"If it was stamped, she could have just dropped it in
the box outside the door," said the clerk, pointing.
"Was it stamped?"

"Er, yes, it was. How stupid of me not to have
thought of that." With a fixed smile on his face, Chris
walked out of the post office. Had Eva's brown envelope been sealed? He couldn't remember. But the
obvious explanation was that she had had several
stamped envelopes to mail, and had placed them in
the larger one to keep them safely together during the
ride into town. At least, that was likely what she
would tell him if he challenged her.

Once he had satisfied himself that Bertoldo wasn't
lurking around corners in Santa Eulalia, Chris walked
the bike up the beach path as far as the Balear River,
deciding on the spur of the moment to return to the old
Roman bridge that Esteban had pointed out to him the

previous morning. The count had been right. The bridge was a masterpiece of ancient architecture. Still relatively intact, its four low, massive arches spanned the river, connecting the four rocky islands that supported it with a structure that looked as though it could handle a heavy automobile.

After admiring the bridge for several minutes Chris headed back in the direction of town, stopping for a moment near a fresh-water spring that bubbled out of the ground only a couple of hundred yards from the sea. Looking up then, he spotted an old stone building at the crest of the hill that overlooked Santa Eulalia and decided to climb up and investigate it.

The road doubled back steeply along the mountain ridge and wound tight circles up the hill, forcing Chris to get off the bike and walk. From this height he had an excellent view of Santa Eulalia's back streets, with their rows of sugar-cube houses that grew dingier and more ramshackle toward the outskirts of town.

The building at the top of the hill turned out to be a church, but its design showed such strong Arabic influences that Chris wondered whether it hadn't at one time been a mosque. He tried the doors, and, discovering that they were locked, sat down on the front steps to admire the scenery.

Suddenly he sensed that he wasn't alone up there. Automatically he tensed, Bertoldo's sharp features coming into focus in his mind's eye as Chris prepared to whirl and confront his antagonist. Then a lizard skittered along a wall and he almost jumped out of his skin.

"Hi, there," said a cheerful voice behind him. "You're not Spanish, are you?"

Chris took three steadying breaths, then rose to his feet with studied casualness and replied, "No, Canadian."

His questioner was Bertoldo's exact opposite—black hair, swarthy skin and a Castilian hooked nose in the middle of an arrogantly handsome face. "That's what I thought," he went on chattily. "With the blond hair you might have been English, although I suppose it's the same thing."

"Not to a Canadian," Chris said softly, but the other man didn't hear him.

"Women!" he sighed. "They love to make fools of us, don't you agree? The one I'm with wanted to take pictures of the cemetery, God alone knows why. Naturally it's locked, and I had to chase down the watchman to borrow the key. And now that I've got it she's disappeared somewhere. By the way, I'm a guide with a travel agency in Ibiza. My name is Ramón Delgado. Are you here with a tour group, also?"

"No, I'm staying with a friend."

Undaunted, Ramón went on, "Well, anytime your friend can't show you around and you'd like to see the sights with a congenial group, just give me a call. Here's my card."

Just then a girl limped around the corner of the church. It was the same one Chris had seen standing in line on the dock, her hair a mass of blond curls and her makeup still more appropriate for a Paris disco than a tour of rustic Ibiza. This time she was wearing a dirndl skirt and matching red peasant blouse, and she waved something in the air as she called out, "I broke my heel!"

Ramón sighed and turned eloquent eyes to Chris

before replying, "I *told* you they weren't walking shoes."

"Well, they're the only ones I brought that go with this outfit," she fumed, drawing nearer without really noticing Chris yet. Meanwhile he was frowning, refusing to believe that two such different women could have the same voice. Even the accent was the same.

"Hello there," Chris ventured, hoping to draw a reaction from her that would identify her one way or the other.

She did a double take, then burst into smiles. "Hello," she caroled. "Didn't I see you on the dock?"

"Didn't I see you on the ship?" Chris rejoined, frowning.

"Oh." Her smile faded, but only for a moment. "Well, how do you like my new look? I think it's fun to change one's appearance from time to time."

"I think I preferred the old look." Chris studied her a moment, and finally reached the conclusion that she was sweet, if a trifle kooky.

"That wasn't the impression I got," Colette said dryly, after letting him have his scrutiny.

"Do you two know each other?" Ramón chimed in brightly. "Wonderful— you can walk down to the bus together while I return this key to the watchman."

When the guide had disappeared around the side of the building, Chris said, "I tried to apologize to you before the ship docked but I couldn't find you."

"I guess because you weren't looking for a blonde."

"It was rude of me to walk away from you that night, no matter how much I had on my mind. I'm sorry," he said earnestly.

She shrugged and smiled at him. "It's all right. I

hope that whatever was bothering you is straightened out now."

"More or less," he lied. "Why?"

"Well, if you've got your act together I'd like to show you off to the other girls on the tour."

Chris laughed. "You must be desperate."

"Don't joke about it," she warned him. "We out-number the guys four to one."

Uttering a low whistle, Chris remarked, "I *like* those odds."

"Not so fast. First I want to know some facts about you, Mr. Laval."

Chris saluted her smartly. "Yes, ma'am."

"How old are you?"

"I'll be thirty in September."

Colette broke into a grin. "So you can be trusted for another few months. What are you studying?"

"I'd better level with you," he said sheepishly. "I'm not a student. I teach Spanish at the University of Paris." Her eyes wide, she stepped back to appraise him and Chris teased, "What's the matter? Don't associate professors show off well?"

"Quite the opposite, they show off *too* well," she told him with an impish grin. "And I don't want to wind up sharing you with anyone."

"Why, thank you, ma'am," Chris drawled, and tipped an imaginary hat. "That's downright flattering to hear."

"Come on," she said, laughing, "walk me to the bus."

Chris wondered how he could have missed seeing a tour bus at the top of the hill, until he saw where it was parked. The driver must have been a camouflage expert during World War II, for he'd pulled the rickety-looking vehicle right into a grove of almond trees, where it was concealed on all sides by tree trunks that matched its coloring perfectly.

Suddenly Colette turned toward him and said impulsively, "Come back to the hotel with us. There's an absolutely marvelous little stretch of beach behind the swimming pool where we can walk and . . . and talk."

One look into those pleading hazel eyes and Chris willingly surrendered his bike to the driver, who produced a length of rope to fasten it to the luggage rack on the roof. Sitting beside Colette at the back of the bus, Chris began once again to feel happy and relaxed as the group of students around him traded quips and teased one another.

As the ancient vehicle executed a laborious turn and set off slowly down the hill, however, he remembered that he was working as an agent for the French government. Did he have the right to follow a personal inclination as long as his assignment was uncompleted? More to the point, did he have the right to become involved with a woman, thus possibly dragging her into his dilemma and complicating—perhaps endangering—two lives instead of just one?

She mustn't get involved, he promised himself.

Stealing a glance at Colette's smiling face, he felt a pang of regret for the moment when he would have to take his leave of her, perhaps never see her again. He couldn't tell her why, either. Would she ever forgive him for abandoning her a second time?

Colette hadn't lied about the beach. Descending the crude wooden steps from the raised patio around the swimming pool, she led him onto an expanse of fine white sand, fringed by the same sort of rocks Chris had seen at Santa Eulalia, and dotted with fragments of seashell. The wind was bracing and laced with salt, and the leaden sea under a suddenly lowering sky looked truly vast and menacing. Chris wasn't surprised to notice that he and Colette were the only people on the beach.

"Tell me about yourself," she said.

"There isn't much to tell. I come from a typical middle-class family comprised mostly of teachers. Though I do have a second cousin who runs a printing shop, and an uncle who sells cars in Montreal."

"That isn't what I mean," she scolded him with a smile. "Where in Canada are you from?"

"Saint-Boniface, Manitoba," he replied.

"The prairies." She nodded sagely. "That explains a great deal about you."

"Really?" Chris said, glancing skeptically at her.

"Yes. People who live in mountainous areas learn to accept disorder, if not of their own making then of the sort that the mountains send them in the form of rock slides and avalanches. But flatlanders like things to be just so."

"Are you implying that I'm pernickety, ma'am?" he asked, amused.

"No, I'm saying it straight out, you ought to loosen up a little, raise some hell once in a while. Do you a world of good," she declared. "Look at you—you're so tense your face is twitching."

"I'm just trying not to laugh at you."

"Good. I like to be taken seriously, especially by interesting men."

Chris felt a rush of affection for this bold, almost childlike young woman with her outspoken opinions and her sparkling sense of humor. *God, how I'm going to miss her*, he thought with a curious ache in the pit of his stomach.

Suddenly it was raining. Huge drops landed with audible thuds on the packed sand. Laughing, Chris and Colette raced toward the cabanas just off the beach.

"It wasn't supposed to do that," Chris declared when they were safely inside one of the little cubicles. "The weather report said—"

"Only flatlanders pay attention to the weather report," Colette teased him.

With an exasperated gesture Chris sat down on the shelf that served as a seat. It was just wide enough for one, and Colette said happily as she settled onto his lap, "I *wondered* why you brought me here."

Chris tried to suppress the sudden surge of desire that coursed through him. He'd never have a better time than this to tell Colette he couldn't see her again.

This was when he was supposed to tell her in his best man-of-the-world voice that he would be too busy to see her anymore, suggest without saying it that there might be another, older woman in his life, propose cheerfully that they might get together back in Paris. "Colette," he began nervously, "I have something to tell you. . . . "

All at once his mind was a blank, and he was aware only of her tantalizing perfume and the yielding softness of her in his arms. She was warm and fitted so neatly against him that he was embracing her almost before he knew what was happening. As she placed her arm over his shoulders and rested her head against his, her ripe young lips drew close enough to be kissed. . . . *No! It wasn't supposed to happen this way!*

"Colette," he began again.

"What is it?" she murmured. There was a smile in her voice.

"This . . . this rain is liable to go on forever, and I have to be getting back. Let's go back to the hotel."

With a disappointed sigh, Colette stood up and followed him at a run into the hotel.

"Where's my bike?" he asked once they were out of the rain.

"Probably in the rack out front," Colette told him. "But you aren't going to ride all the way back to Santa Eulalia in this rain, are you?"

"I'll be all right." A cold shower was just what he needed at that moment. . . .

Chapter 7

"Is that someone at the door?"

Chris put down his fork and listened. The rapping wasn't loud, but it was persistent.

"That *is* someone at the front door," Esteban repeated with surprise. "Who could be calling at this early hour of the morning?"

"I'm coming, I'm coming!" Soledad called impatiently as she swept past the breakfast table, wiping her hands on her apron and muttering to herself.

Slowly Chris resumed eating, straining between mouthfuls to hear snatches of the conversation that was taking place at the door.

Suddenly Soledad was back. "Someone for Mr. Laval," she reported disapprovingly. "A young tourist woman wanting him to join her."

Chris nearly choked on his coffee. A young tourist woman—that had to be Colette. But he knew he hadn't told her where he was staying. How had she found him?

Esteban shot him a quizzical look as Chris leaped up from the table. After the tale he'd told about the shy Ibizan beauty, what must the count be thinking of him! But, as Roig had said with such an eloquent sigh, those were the breaks of the game. Perhaps one day Chris could explain everything to him.

Colette was waiting outside the door, at the head of a small tribe of happily chattering young people. Chris noted with some pleasure that her face was free of makeup this morning, although she still wore the blond wig. Like the other students she was in slacks and a pullover sweater, with a healthy flush in her cheeks.

"At last!" she cried. "Are you surprised?"

"I'm astonished," he declared truthfully. "How did you find me?"

"That's unimportant," she replied coyly. "Will you come boating with us?"

"We rented a skiff from the marina in Ibiza," one of the boys chimed in enthusiastically. "It's a gorgeous ride around the point."

"You've got to come," cried one of the girls. "We hiked all the way up here from Santa Eulalia to invite you."

"Circulate, do all the things that tourists do," Roig had told him. Chris gazed smilingly into Colette's fresh-looking young face and rationalized away his decision not to see her again. What harm could come to her when she was with a group of obviously innocent students? "Let me get a sweater," he said.

Esteban had let him keep the green turtleneck to use, and Chris was still struggling into it when he re-emerged from the house.

Colette fell into step beside him as they set off down

the hill. "You probably saved my life, you know," she informed him. "It was my idea to hike up to the house and call on you. If you'd refused to come out, I think they would have lynched me."

Chris laughed. Then, "Seriously, how did you know where to find me?"

"You're such a flatlander," she teased him. "You simply hate an unanswered question. I remembered seeing an older man meet you on the dock Sunday morning. Ramón recognized my description of him and happened to know the count's address, and I took a chance that you'd be there."

"What if you'd been wrong?"

"I would have had a lot of ruffled feathers to smooth. This is a long way to go on a fool's errand."

They'd beached the skiff on a narrow strand under a grove of weather-beaten old pines, within sight of the rocky beach Chris had visited the previous afternoon. Smelling faintly of fish, the boat held them all comfortably, and two oars on each side kept it moving steadily away from shore and around the sharp spur of land that jutted like a thorn into the sea.

One of the boys had brought along a pair of binoculars, which soon began making the rounds of the boat as everyone clamored for a closer look at the shore. Chris's turn came just as the skiff rounded the point, and as he focused the glasses on a clump of twisted olive trees he suddenly realized that he was looking at a scattering of small huts, interspersed with trees and empty easels. No, one of the easels held a canvas, the one set up next to an isolated agave tree.

Just then the painter behind the easel stood up and gazed intently in the direction of Ibiza. Gulping hard, Chris stared at the artist, searching for the line of a scar as he reconstructed the jawline under the man's thick blond beard. He was sure now. It was Bertoldo.

"My turn," said the girl beside Chris, reaching for the glasses. "What's so interesting out there, anyway?"

"Nothing," he replied in what he hoped was a casual voice. "I just thought I recognized someone."

The girl stared through the binoculars. "That's the same guy we saw there yesterday, when we were with the tour. I tried to talk to him, but he doesn't speak Spanish or French."

"Oh, that one?" remarked the boy sitting ahead of her. "He speaks German. We talked a little about his work, and I don't think he's a professional artist, in spite of the airs he puts on. He's probably an insurance salesman or something, and when his vacation is over he'll step out of his paint-spattered corduroys, put on a gray flannel suit and go home to his wife and two children in the suburbs."

Not quite, Chris thought grimly. *Not quite*. So Bertoldo was hiding out in the artists' colony? It was apparently a tourist spot, and that could make capturing him difficult . . . but the details were up to Roig, Chris decided. Now all he had to do was get word to Jondalitx at the dig.

"Why don't we row over to Cala Llonga?" he suggested artlessly. "It's on the way to Ibiza, and I understand it's quite an impressive sight from the water. And I'd appreciate it if you'd drop me off there, because I promised my friend Esteban I'd meet him at his archeological site."

"Sure, why not?" said one of the girls brightly, and the others agreed.

But as Chris took his turn at the oars he heard one of

the boys moan, "I'm exhausted. A four-mile hike and now all this rowing . . . I came here for a *rest*, for God's sake!"

You and me both, friend, Chris thought ruefully, oblivious to the puzzled, hurt expression on Colette's face.

CHRIS COULDN'T BELIEVE HIS LUCK. As he trudged up from the beach at Cala Llonga there was only one man at the entrance to the dig, dumping out a pailful of dirt. It was Jondalitx.

Hunching low behind a rock, Chris called out in a hoarse whisper, "Jondalitx! Over here!" and the foreman ambled over with studied casualness. "Tell Roig I've seen Bertoldo," Chris whispered. "He's posing as an artist at the colony down the coast. He's grown a beard, and he's wearing brown corduroy pants, a checked shirt and a straw hat. He was there yesterday, too."

"All right," replied Jondalitx tersely. "I can tell you what Roig's reply will be. The colony's a tourist trap. With all those people around we can't make a move. You'll have to get him someplace more private."

"You're kidding!" Chris shot back, nearly breaking into a normal voice. "Roig didn't say anything about my getting more involved. Besides, Bertoldo knows who I am—he's been following me for weeks. If I so much as show my face he'll know something's up."

Jondalitx shrugged. "That's your problem, friend," he said dryly, then went back to work.

Chris spent several long minutes behind his rock, feeling old and weary. He didn't want to participate personally in Bertoldo's capture. There were any number of ruses he might have been able to try if the

man had never seen him before. But it was a waste of
time to dwell on them. Somehow Chris had to lure
Bertoldo to an out-of-the-way spot without showing
his face. What a trick that was going to be!

There was a message waiting for him when he got
back to the house: "Bring your swimsuit down to the
hotel after lunch. Colette." Even though he hated
himself for it, Chris knew he was going to meet her.
The long walk home from the site, while his thoughts
chased each other around in his head, had produced
only one workable scheme for carrying out his assignment. It was a plan he detested because it meant
using Colette, and he'd already promised himself he
wouldn't get her involved. Damn! Why did life have to
be so complicated?

"You're awfully quiet," Esteban remarked halfway
through lunch. "Didn't you enjoy your boat ride?"

Chris glanced up at him in surprise.

"You were seen by some fishermen," the count
went on with an indulgent smile. "This is a small
place, Christopher, and people have little to do besides talk, so word travels very quickly. Your coloring
makes you conspicuous, you know. If you were
darker hardly anybody would notice where you went
or what you did."

Chris pressed his lips together for a moment. Had
someone also seen him get off the skiff at Cala Llonga?
Apparently not, or Esteban would have mentioned his
failure to stop in at the excavation. Chris would have
to be more careful in future. *Good grief, if it isn't the spies
watching you it's the gossip-hungry locals!*

Colette was waiting for him in a lounging chair
beside the hotel's heart-shaped swimming pool. She
had on the briefest bikini he had ever seen. As soon as

he stepped through the door from the lobby, she began posing for him, fluttering her eyelashes comically as she assumed various outlandish positions. Her physical charms were considerable, but it was her blond wig Chris was most interested in—he was relieved to see she hadn't yet decided to switch back to her brunette look.

"Where's your swimsuit?" she asked as he strode over to her.

"I didn't bring it," he replied. "I thought of something better for us to do this afternoon."

She smiled coyly. "What is it?"

"I thought we'd take a taxi over to the artists' colony."

"Unless you're an art critic or interested in buying, there's very little to see there," Colette told him with a disappointed edge to her voice. "Wouldn't you rather go for a swim?"

Chris shook his head. "I *am* interested in buying, you see, only . . . only there's a hitch. I need you to help me out."

"Oh?"

Licking his lower lip nervously, Chris leaned forward and explained, "Remember that artist we saw from the boat this morning—the German? On the way back from the dig, Esteban and I detoured through the artists' colony and we saw some of his work. Esteban liked it so much that I decided to commission a painting for him, as a gift to thank him for his hospitality. But I want it to be a complete surprise, and that's my problem. This island is like a small town—if someone conspicuous, like me, or you in that wig, does anything at all, everyone for miles around is discussing it in no time flat. If I commission that painting it won't be a surprise. But if you were to approach the artist, without your wig. . . . " Chris let his voice fade out suggestively.

"You want me to be your go-between?" Colette looked rather dubious.

"You'd only have to do it once, I promise." *Once has to be enough*, he added mentally, *or I'm in trouble.*

"All right," she sighed at last. "If I do you this favor, *then* will you come for a swim with me?"

"Of course!"

Chris told the taxi driver to let them off a half-mile from the artists' colony. When the rickety old cab had turned around and was out of sight down the road he directed Colette to a thick clump of bushes and stood guard while she changed. At his instructions, she had left the hotel wearing the wig and the same garish makeup he'd seen her in on the dock. She had also stuffed into her spacious handbag a dress and a pair of shoes that she hadn't yet had occasion to wear on Ibiza. If Colette found his precautions unusual, she hadn't commented on them. Chris rather suspected that she was caught up in this cloak-and-dagger escapade, relishing it with childish enthusiasm. Fervently he hoped that she wouldn't relish it enough to want to repeat it.

The young lady who emerged from behind the copse was elegant and demure in a blue cotton shirtwaist and a pair of white ankle-strap shoes. Her light brown hair was tied at the nape of her neck with a blue velvet ribbon, and she wore only a touch of pale pink lipstick on her smiling lips. She was ravishing. For a second Chris couldn't think of anything to say. He was content just to stand there and admire her.

"I gather you approve," she remarked happily. "Well, tell me what you want me to say to this artist."

Shaking off his inertia, Chris replied, "Tell him it's for you. You want him to paint the old Roman bridge as seen from under the new one. You'll pay him whatever he charges. You want him to start tomorrow, since the weather is good and you'll be leaving . . . oh, say Saturday. Leave your things here with me. How's your German?"

"I got As in all my oral tests," she informed him archly.

Chris smiled. "I'll be waiting right here for you."

As he watched her walk away from him with a confident swing to her stride, Chris felt a pang of guilt. To trap Bertoldo he'd first had to trap Colette—trick her into actually setting the agent up for him. She couldn't possibly know what the stakes were. For that matter, did Chris know much more? All Roig had said was that Bertoldo was the spy who'd been following Chris. He'd never explained *why* an espionage organization had suddenly taken an interest in the politically naive languages professor from Manitoba. After giving it a second's thought, Chris decided that Roig was right: he probably was better off not knowing any of the details.

Forty-five minutes later Colette was back, smiling triumphantly.

"Mission accomplished!" she caroled. "He'll be happy to paint the picture. He's agreed to be under the new bridge tomorrow morning at nine."

"He didn't seem . . . suspicious at all?" Chris asked carefully.

Colette shrugged. "Suspicious of what? He wanted

my name and address so he could deliver the painting,
which is normal. But I told him I was staying in San
Antonio Abad, on the other side of the island, and I
gave him a false name, too. You really ought to explain
the situation to him before the poor guy goes running
all the way over there and figures he's been had."
Reaching for her handbag, she added, "Why not
tomorrow morning? I'd like to find out what's so
special about that old Roman bridge." Then she disappeared into the thicket to change.

At once Chris's mind began to race. He had to get
word to Jondalitx. It was nearly four o'clock—would
he still be at the dig? By Chris's calculations, the site
was less than two miles away. Somehow, that distance was much less dismaying after his bike ride
home from Ibiza in the rain. If he and Colette walked
up to the dig, they wouldn't be far from a bus stop on
the main road. Then Chris could return to the hotel
with her, pick up his bicycle and ride back. That
sounded all right, if he could get Colette to agree to it.

When she finally re-emerged from the bushes, once
more in jeans, wig and makeup, Chris smiled win-
ningly at her and said, "On the way back to Ibiza, do
you mind if we stop at Cala Llonga for a short while? I
have something to tell Esteban."

Cocking her head to one side, Colette gave him a
strange look before saying yes.

JONDALITX HADN'T BEEN AT THE EXCAVATION. As he
pedaled furiously along the main road toward Santa
Eulalia, Chris's mind flooded with plans and sur-
mises. Perhaps he could telephone Jondalitx. No, the
vast majority of the people on the island had no
phone. If Soledad would tell him where her nephew

lived, Chris might be able to arrange to go for a little stroll between tea time and dinner . . . unless it rained. Even if it didn't, Chris realized, he'd be compromising Jondalitx's effectiveness as a contact by alerting his aunt to the fact that Chris wanted to see him. Urgently.

Good grief, what now? Contact Roig directly? But how, when the only places he'd seen the man were on the dock and on board the cruiser in the harbor?

As each possibility was rejected, Chris felt a strange numbing weariness wash over him, so that by the time he reached the front door of Esteban's house he felt as though he'd pedaled twelve *hundred* miles. This was ridiculous, he told himself sternly. He wasn't a trained agent; he wasn't even a willing one. How could anyone expect him to do the impossible? And why the hell wouldn't his knees stop shaking?

As he stepped through the living-room door, Chris froze in disbelief. The windows in the room looked out onto the patio, and there, bent head-to-head over a shrub heavy with white blossoms, were Esteban and Jondalitx. Chris returned to the hallway, afraid of being seen before he was ready.

There was little chance of drawing Jondalitx aside for a whispered conversation. Suddenly Chris remembered the small memo sheets on Eva's desk. As stealthily as a burglar, he peered around the doorway of the office before entering it, but Eva had already finished for the day and gone home. Chris took one of the small pieces of paper and wrote on it, "Tomorrow, 9 a.m., under new bridge." Then he folded the paper until it was small enough to conceal in the palm of his hand. At last he was ready to venture out onto the patio.

"Ah, Christopher, there you are," said Esteban, glancing up at the sound of Chris's footsteps. "You know Jondalitx, of course."

Stiffly Chris nodded, then realized he'd missed an opportunity to shake the foreman's hand and pass on the note, and felt like kicking himself.

"What do you think of this *sempervirens*?" Esteban went on. "It's one of the few flowering evergreens, possibly the only such shrub on the island."

Chris gulped hard. A handshake was out. He'd just have to find some way of slipping Jondalitx the note.

"Christopher?" Esteban was staring strangely at him. "Are you feeling all right? You look pale."

"I'm fine," Chris protested. "Really, just fine."

"If you say so," the count said and returned to his examination of the shrub.

As Esteban turned away momentarily, Chris reached out with his free hand and tapped Jondalitx lightly on the arm. The foreman nodded, then remarked, "Look, *señor*, that blossom seems wilted."

"Which one?" While the count was inspecting the bottom of the bush, the note changed hands.

There, Chris thought with a sigh of relief, he'd done his part. Now it was up to Roig and his men to make the actual capture, after which, if he was lucky, Chris would never have to have anything to do with French Intelligence again.

THE FOLLOWING MORNING, as they had agreed before parting, Chris rode the bicycle into Ibiza to call for Colette. He deliberately waited until nine o'clock to leave the house, however, figuring that Colette would insist on visiting the bridge, and not wanting to arrive in the thick of the battle. He was right on both counts.

Colette nagged him until he consented to take her there, and when they left their bikes at the side of the road and peered over the railing of the new bridge, the rocky bank below was empty. There was no one there.

Chris feigned surprised disappointment. "It looks as though that artist forgot about us," he remarked.

"And Germans are usually so meticulous and punctual," Colette said. "I wonder what happened to— Hey, wait a minute!" she cried suddenly, and pointed to something shiny that lay among the rocks. "What's that?"

Chris had a stomach-churning hunch what it was, and did his best to detract her from it. "It's probably just an empty tin or something that somebody threw away. Shall we ride to the top of the ridge?"

"It's too small to be a tin," she declared stubbornly.

"It's litter," he told her impatiently. "Let's forget about it and go look at the Roman bridge."

"Not until we find out what that thing is." Colette turned expectant eyes on his face, finally shrugging with annoyance and saying, "All right, then, if you won't climb down there and get it, I will."

As she rounded the railing of the bridge Chris heaved a resigned sigh and called out, "Okay, okay, I'll fetch you the damn thing!"

Slowly making his way down the steep river bank, he already knew what he would find—a half-used tube of oil paint. He was tempted to throw it right into the river, but even as he turned that plan over in his mind, Colette called down to him, "It's a tube of paint, isn't it? I knew it was."

"It doesn't have to be his, you know," Chris called back. "The island is full of painters, and this is a popular view of the old bridge."

"But it might be his," she insisted. Chris threw his arms up in surrender and began climbing back toward her as she went on relentlessly, "And if it *is* his, then he's either the fastest or the laziest artist I've ever met. He's certainly the most absent-minded—this stuff costs money, and the tube can't be more than half-empty." She reached for the paint, but Chris dropped it into his jacket pocket.

"Why don't we ride down to the artists' colony and return this to him?" he suggested with sudden inspiration.

"Oh, so now you've decided that it belongs to him after all?" she commented sarcastically.

Chris saw anger mixed with bewilderment in her eyes. "I thought women weren't supposed to be logical," he joked, trying to ease the tension.

"Rubbish!" she snapped. "And you're hardly the one to claim that men are logical, especially after this morning."

"What?"

She started counting off on her fingers. "First you spotted that German fellow through the field glasses yesterday morning, then suddenly you had to be put ashore at Cala Llonga to meet your friend. Yesterday afternoon you had some cooked-up excuse for sending me to order a painting instead of going yourself—"

"It wasn't an excuse!" he interrupted.

"—and on the way back took us two miles out of our way so you could say something to your friend at Cala Llonga, leaving me standing with the donkey—"

"It's a mule."

"I don't care! The point is that you tucked me carefully out of the way so I couldn't see what was going on. You wouldn't even introduce me to your friend. And now, this paint tube.... You knew what it was as soon as I spotted it, didn't you? But you didn't want me to find out, so you tried to drag me away to see the Roman bridge. Why, Chris? What's going on?"

A line about flatlanders rose automatically to his lips, but he stifled it. "I... wish I could tell you, Colette. I honestly do."

She turned her troubled gaze to the empty river bank. "Why do I have the feeling that you know exactly what happened here this morning?" she said quietly.

Chris put a gentle hand on her shoulder. "Trust me, Colette," he murmured. "You don't want to be involved."

She essayed a brave smile. "What are you, some kind of secret agent?" she quipped, but there were tears in her eyes. "Just my luck, with all the gorgeous men on Ibiza I have to get mixed up with a spy!"

"I'm not a spy," he said emphatically.

"Then what are you?" she demanded. "A criminal?"

"Not that, either. I'm just someone who fell into a mess," he muttered.

Restlessly, she turned and walked over to the bicycles.

"I'm going back to the hotel," she said.

"I'll ride with you."

"No, please, Chris." Her eyes pleaded with him. "I need to be alone right now ... need to sort things out."

As he stood watching her pedal out of sight down the road, Chris had the heart-wrenching feeling that he'd just lost something very precious to him.

Chapter 8

Chris wandered aimlessly for the next couple of hours. He felt like an unstrung puppet. Now that his assignment for Roig had been completed he no longer had to impersonate a tourist. And with Colette withdrawn in hurt confusion, for who knew how long, he felt more alone than he had ever felt in his life. Totally at loose ends, not knowing what he wanted to do and hardly caring whether he did anything, Chris pedaled along the unpaved road, his mind in turmoil.

His two previous clandestine trips to the dig had spoiled any chance of enjoyment he might derive from the place this morning. The bridge, too, held only the unsavory memory of the part he'd played in Bertoldo's capture, and the very thought of venturing into the artists' colony depressed him. Ibiza meant either narrow streets and Dolores, or large hotel complexes and Colette. And if he went anywhere near the marina or the fishermen's dock he might run into Roig and find himself conscripted for another dirty assignment.

Suddenly Chris was seized with guilt. Colette would be right to hate him after the soulless way he'd used her to set Bertoldo up. With a pang of longing he recalled the anguished expression in her eyes just before they parted. She may not have known what she was doing at the time she'd lured the agent to the bridge, but she certainly suspected it now. Convinced that he'd lost her forever, Chris gritted his teeth and pedaled even harder. What an empty place the world had suddenly become. . . .

Fields and groves of trees passed him in a blur. Water appeared on his left, then vanished behind a rise in the terrain. Indifferent to the scenery, Chris sank into nightmarish speculation as the wind whipped unheeded at his perspiring face.

If Bertoldo had been killed, then Chris was an accessory to the murder. What would Roig do, he wondered. Would he now get rid of an unwilling accomplice who knew too much? Or would he blackmail him with the information to squeeze one more assignment out of him . . . and another . . . and another . . . ? No matter what happened, Chris was the loser.

So what the devil was he still doing on Ibiza? *I should have run like hell to Canada when I had the chance*, he decided.

Chris wasn't sure how it happened, but the next thing he knew he was approaching Esteban's front door just in time for lunch. Too weary and dejected to care about amenities, Chris slung his jacket over his chair instead of leaving it on the coatrack inside the front door. Not even Soledad's reproachful stares could penetrate his gloom.

"You look so unhappy, Christopher. Is there anything I can do for you?" Esteban asked as they sat down to lunch.

Chris shook his head. "Colette and I have had a . . . falling out. If you don't mind, Esteban, I'd rather not discuss it."

"Of course, my friend," said the count sympathetically. "Perhaps you would enjoy a tour by mule cart of this half of the island after lunch. We can stop in San Miguel or Portinatx for Maundy Thursday mass."

"What about the dig?"

"The dig can wait a few days longer. It occurs to me that I've been a very poor host. After all, you're here at my invitation, and yet I've hardly spent any time with you at all. This weekend I'll try to remedy that."

Chris nodded and smiled in spite of himself. Esteban was such a devout Catholic that they'd probably wind up spending the entire weekend in church. But anything was better than moping around and thinking about Colette and Bertoldo.

Eva was so quiet that her presence at the table was scarcely noticed until Chris accidentally picked up his jacket upside down. The paint tube he'd found at the bridge fell out of his pocket and landed with a thud on the floor at her feet. "Where did you get that?" she gasped.

Chris decided to tell the truth. "I found it just under the new bridge on the Balear River," he said offhandedly. "Why?"

"Nothing," Eva replied, once more in control of herself. "If you gentlemen will excuse me, I have to run down to the post office."

The two men watched her rush out the door.

THE TIME PASSED very slowly that afternoon and evening. Once the novelty of riding in the mule cart had worn off, Chris had found the tour of small villages a little tedious. Dinner had been uneventful, and after several hours spent reading in his cell-like room, Chris had turned out the light at just past midnight.

About ten minutes later Chris heard a sharp sound at his window. He ignored it. But when it happened twice more he decided to get up and investigate. Carefully he opened the window, and found Dolores standing outside, shivering in her thin shawl.

"Dolores!" he whispered in astonishment. "What are you doing here at this hour?"

"Roig sent me to get you," she replied.

"Forget it," Chris told her harshly. "I'm not available."

"Listen to me," she urged him. "Bertoldo cracked under questioning. He admitted hiding some secret documents and microfilms under the floor of an old farmhouse not far from here. You have to come with me, Mr. Laval. I was the only one Roig could send, and this job requires a man's strength."

"Why didn't Roig go himself?"

"He's not here. He had to leave immediately on an emergency." As Chris still hesitated she said exasperatedly, "Look, do you think I'd have bothered you if I didn't need your help?"

Chris thought for a moment. "All you want me to do is pry up a few floorboards?" he repeated.

"Yes. I've brought a crowbar and a couple of flashlights—they're in the basket of my bicycle. Will you come?" she pleaded.

He sighed. "All right. Give me a minute to get dressed and I'll meet you out front."

Once he'd slipped into his blue jeans and the green turtleneck Chris groped for his socks and shoes, then carried them through the darkened house to the little vestibule, where he paused to finish dressing. When he stepped out the front door, Dolores was waiting for him with two bicycles.

"I took one out of the shed for you," she whispered. "The count's bedroom light is still on, and I saw a shadow move behind the drapes, so we'll have to be careful. Follow me."

Neither of the bikes had lights, but there was a sliver of moon casting just enough glow to keep Chris going in the right direction as they walked their bicycles down to the road. Once there he had no difficulty following Dolores down the slope, for the odd time he lost her silhouette in the darkness, the gentle whirring of her wheels located her again.

Fifteen minutes later they slowed down and turned onto a well-packed dirt road, riding straight along it until three white buildings appeared on the right, their dingy sides silvered by the moonlight. Dolores veered off the road and stopped, waiting for Chris to pull up alongside her. "It's the middle one," she whispered, pointing.

By now Chris's eyes were accustomed to the darkness, and as they drew closer he saw that these buildings resembled the sugar-cube houses in the poorer sections of Ibiza, with their doors and windows simply holes carved out of their walls. Then Dolores concealed her bike in the shrubbery at the side of the middle building and Chris followed suit, letting her precede him inside.

Slowly their flashlight beams swept around what appeared to be a single large, empty room. It was even reasonably clean, leading one to suppose that it had been abandoned quite recently. Just then Dolores nudged him. "Come help me look," she said in a soft voice. "We have to find a small cross carved into a floorboard."

It was hard work using only their flashlights. After a few eye-straining minutes Chris flicked his beam impatiently across the room, starting as it picked out something shiny on a shelf near the back window.

"Mr. Laval, where are you going?" Dolores asked in a frightened voice.

"If this is what I hope it is . . . . It is!" he exclaimed. "I've found a lantern. That ought to make our work a little easier. Have you brought any matches?"

"No," she replied abruptly.

"Never mind—I think I have some." Sure enough, there was a book of matches in his pocket.

But as he struck the first match Dolores cried out sharply, "No! We've got Bertoldo but not the rest of his gang," she pleaded in a half whisper. "They may be watching this place, and a lantern light would be visible all the way from the main road. Please, Mr. Laval!"

Reluctantly he blew out the flame and heard Dolores sigh with relief in the darkness. "I'd better made a quick check outside and make sure no one is around," she said. "Meanwhile you can start looking again."

Chris had worked his way nearly to the back of the room when he heard a small sound. Expecting Dolores, he peered into the darkness, but could see nothing. A knot tightened in his stomach and his skin began to crawl.

Quickly he reached out and grabbed the crowbar in his free hand. Then he leaped to his feet and swung the beam of his flashlight all around the room, capturing in its glow the figures of three men, one of them holding a gun. Galvanized by the sight of the weapon, Chris hurled the flashlight at it with all his strength, in the same instant lashing out wildly with the crowbar.

He connected with a sickening thud, and there was the crash of a body dropping to the floor. But all at once his arm was trapped in a steely grip and the crowbar was twisted violently from his hand. A moment later his other arm was confined, and Chris felt himself being forced to the ground. How could only two men be doing this, he wondered. It felt as though he were fighting an army single-handedly—they were all over him.

Just as Chris gathered his legs to attempt to spring free, they were knocked out from under him and he landed heavily on the floor, bruising his shoulder painfully. He barely had time to gasp before he was securely pinned down, and to add insult to injury someone roughly grabbed a handful of his hair to hold his head still.

How many were there? Three? A dozen? As Chris lay helplessly on the ground, heaving great sobbing breaths, his thoughts turned to the ally who should have tried to warn him. What had happened to Dolores? Had they quietly disposed of her outside, or was she waiting around the corner of the building with a loaded revolver? He didn't dare mention her name, if these were Bertoldo's men, for fear of ruining her element of surprise. If only these assailants hadn't been so efficient! Chris was almost ready to believe that they could see in the dark, like cats.

"Who . . . the hell . . . are you?" he muttered

through gritted teeth as his immobilized muscles began to cramp.

They refused to answer him, but the man nearest his head chuckled deep in his throat. Suddenly someone else entered the room. Chris heard the metallic click of the door opening just as a large cloth bag was thrown over his head. There was the scrape and hissing of a match being struck, and Chris guessed that the lantern was being lit.

"Where do you want to do it?" one of the men muttered to another.

"Just hold his left leg still," came the reply.

"What are you doing?" Chris demanded, stiffening against the many hands pinning him to the floor.

"Just relax and be grateful that we were instructed not to hurt you, fella," warned a rumbling voice near his left ear.

Chris felt a pin-prick in his left ankle, and then the world winked out.

CHRIS AWAKENED TO FIND the sunlight hitting his face like a sledge-hammer. He cursed silently to himself. *They've done it to me again.* His eyeballs were on fire and there was an insistent throbbing pain in his temples that washed halfway down his jaw and across the back of his neck. As he raised himself slowly to a sitting position and looked around, he realized that he was on Esteban's patio, only several paces from the back door. The sun was already up, and he could hear and smell breakfast being prepared.

Had he dreamed the entire fantastic episode? Had he come out here for some air before retiring, slipped and hit his head and hallucinated the whole thing?

There was one way to find out. Rolling up the cuff of his left pant leg, Chris saw the coin-sized purple stain of a bruise around the puncture mark on his left ankle. So it was real. They'd drugged him and then let him go—again. But why? What was the purpose of this insane cat-and-mouse game? Painfully he got to his feet, wincing at the rush of pain to his shoulder.

"Ah, there you are, Christopher!" Startled, Chris whirled and saw the count standing on the patio behind him. "The air is certainly bracing at this hour of the morning, isn't it?"

Chris tried not to grimace as Esteban patted him on the shoulder. "Yes, it is," he agreed in a faint voice, his head pounding unmercifully.

"My, you're not at your best first thing in the morning, are you?" Esteban laughed. "I have to apologize, Christopher. I wanted to spend the entire weekend showing you my beautiful Ibiza, but there's more trouble up at the dig and I have to leave right after breakfast if I want to make it to mass later on. Can you forgive me?"

"Sure," Chris replied with a faint smile. "That's what friends are for."

"I hope the air has given you an appetite, by the way. Soledad is an excellent cook at any time, but Easter brings out the genius in her. She really fussed over breakfast this morning."

Chris groaned inwardly. He was in no condition to appreciate a fine cuisine. All he wanted was an unending stream of hot black coffee to silence the percussion section in his head. Soledad would not be happy with him.

After a quick shower that made him feel almost

human again Chris returned to the dining room. Refusing to take no for an answer, the housekeeper brought out a breakfast plate for him. "Even if you don't feel hungry now," she declared over his protestations, "if it sits there and stares at you long enough maybe you'll try some of it."

Chris turned to Esteban for support, but the count only shrugged and smiled helplessly. So the food sat there in front of him, getting colder and less appetizing by the minute while Chris fought off his nausea by drinking cup after cup of strong black coffee. At last Soledad came and took it away, muttering darkly under her breath about crazy foreigners.

About an hour after Esteban had left for the excavation site, there was a knock at the front door. Chris had been sitting in the living room leafing idly through a magazine. Now he moved to the hallway to see who was arriving, and was a little surprised when Soledad opened the door to Eva Tirso, as formally dressed as she had been on the previous Sunday.

"What, working on Good Friday? What about mass?" he teased her.

"I've already been," Eva replied coolly. "I just have a few odds and ends to take care of in the office. I'm off until Tuesday, and I didn't want to leave anything dangling until then." Then, excusing herself, she strode into the office and closed the door, leaving Chris to return with a sigh to the living room. About five minutes later the typewriter began to chatter, stopping after another fifteen or twenty minutes. Chris heard the office door open and close again, and then Eva appeared in the living room, followed by Soledad carrying a coffee tray.

There were two cups on the tray, but Soledad warned her, "Don't let him have any of your coffee—he's had seven cups already this morning!"

With one of her rare smiles, Eva commented, "Caffeine addict?"

"I find it works wonders for my . . . headaches," Chris replied with a rueful grin. "Do you live nearby?"

"Just past the first curve on the road to Santa Eulalia. I rent a small house." Eva sipped her coffee and sighed appreciatively.

"That must make things very convenient for you," remarked Chris.

Suddenly her expression darkened. "What do you mean by that?"

Chris was startled by her vehemence. *Now what have I said*, he wondered. "I didn't mean anything at all," he said hastily. "But in large cities it's not uncommon to have to travel several miles to get from home to one's place of employment. You're fortunate to have found a place that's walking distance from yours. That was all I meant."

Eva stared into her lap, her cheeks pink, although whether with anger on embarrassment Chris couldn't tell. "Forgive me, Mr. Laval," she murmured. "I . . . I don't know what came over me."

Just then there was another knock at the door, and a moment later Soledad appeared, wearing a disapproving look. "That young tourist woman is back," she said.

Chris felt his heart leap in his chest. "Colette?" he asked. "Send her in, please!"

Eva stood up then and straightened her skirt. "I'd better get back to my typewriter," she announced and returned to the office.

When Colette appeared in the living room doorway a moment later, in blue slacks and a matching sweater, blond wig and makeup, she looked distinctly uncomfortable. "Chris," she began, "I've come to apologize."

"You don't have to, you know," he told her earnestly. "I'm the one who—" he gulped hard and picked his words carefully "—who wasn't completely open with you."

"Can you be open with me now?" she asked in a hopeful voice.

"No," he replied, sighing miserably. "I'm sorry."

She pursed her lips for a moment. "Can you at least tell me whether the artist's safe?"

Chris shook his head regretfully. "I don't know that myself."

"I really believe you don't," she said with mild surprise. Then, "Chris, are we friends?"

This was it—the moment when he could set her free from the intrigue that surrounded his life. The previous night's experience had shattered his foolish illusions that he had some control over his destiny. More, it had shown him that he might never be safe again. The nightmare was far from over for him. They could come for him anywhere, anytime—and he couldn't do anything about it. But Colette didn't have to share his ordeal. If he rejected her now she'd be free and clear. All he had to do was send her away....

"Are we friends?" she repeated, bewilderment in her eyes.

He made the mistake of looking directly into her wide hazel eyes . . . and was lost before he knew what happened. "If you want us to be," he heard himself saying.

"Oh, I do!" she cried. "Yesterday morning at the bridge I ran away because I was scared. I'm a flatlander at heart, I guess, and I resented your secretiveness. Actually, I guess I should say I was frightened, too. We students talk a great deal about being liberal-minded and judging people on their own merits, but we're products of a society that teaches us that it's wrong to give your trust to anyone who doesn't respect its boundaries. As soon as I realized that you were possibly operating beyond the pale, so to speak, then all the things that had made me like you were suddenly overshadowed, and I came unglued. But I've thought about it and decided that I don't care what you do for a living, Chris. You're you and . . . I like you," she concluded breathlessly.

"Are you finished?" he asked wryly. "What I do for a living is teach Spanish—believe it or not—at a university that could hardly be described as being 'beyond the pale.' And I certainly am not. Are we straight on that now?"

"Yes," she murmured.

"And you're filled with remorse because you probably think you let me down yesterday, but you didn't. You were just being honest, with me and with yourself, about your feelings. If I'd been that forthright earlier on—" he shook his head "—I wouldn't be in the mess I'm in now."

"Chris, I . . . is there anything I can do to help?" she asked timidly, and reached out to touch his sleeve.

Chris gazed into her little-girl face and suddenly felt swept away in a rush of tender emotion as his whole body yearned to be close to her. He imagined what it would be like to hold her in his arms and whisper endearments into her ear before sharing with her a kiss that would lift them to heights of passion. . . . He actually took a step toward her before his conscience intervened. A man in his present position had nothing to bring to a relationship, he told himself. There would be no security for him until French Intelligence had finished with him, and possibly not even then if any of Bertoldo's men were left at large.

"Let's go for a walk," he muttered, feeling vaguely dissatisfied with himself.

They tackled the ridge behind the house. In self-defense, Chris kept up a steady patter of witty lines about his students and co-workers, and Colette matched him wisecrack for wisecrack as they made their way up the slippery gravel path to the top. From there they saw almost nothing. The view was blocked by trees on all sides.

"Tell me about yourself," Chris said as they sank down on a fallen log to rest. "What do you want to be? What do you want to do with your life?"

"I want to enjoy it, primarily," she replied with a faint smile. "Eventually I'd like to be a simultaneous translator for some branch of the United Nations, but that isn't for some years yet. And if worse came to worst and nobody else would have me, I could teach."

He made a face at her. "That's the problem," he grumbled. "Teaching standards are going downhill because the profession has become a catch-all for people who would really rather be doing something else."

"Sometimes even a bad teacher is better than no teacher," Colette said quietly.

Touché, Chris thought. She would always surprise him with her perceptiveness. No wonder he lov— liked her. He *liked* her, he told himself sternly.

WHEN CHRIS RETURNED from his walk with Colette—after promising to contact her the next day—the lunch table was set for one. Eva had long since gone home and Esteban had obviously sent word not to expect him.

Soledad stared at him dubiously. "You want coffee for lunch?" she demanded in a dry voice.

Chris chuckled and replied, "No, thank you. I've had my fill of it for today, I think." The fresh air had done wonders for his head, and except for the nagging pain in his shoulder and the slight tenderness in his ankle he felt like a new man.

Soledad brought him a salad and a small plate of *paella con arroz*, a savory mixture of chicken, seafood, vegetables and rice, which smelled so good it made his mouth water. As he tucked into his meal, she told him, "*El Señor* will be home in time to change and go to six-o'clock mass." Then she disappeared into the kitchen.

Left to his own devices for the entire afternoon, Chris thought about going into Ibiza to track down Dolores to find out what happened to her the night before—that is if she wasn't now a prisoner. But things hadn't changed—she was just as inaccessible as before, and Chris was leery at this point of attracting undue attention to himself by hanging around town hoping to catch a glimpse of her. After all, just because he had been lucky enough—or unlucky enough—in the past to run into her within minutes of arriving in town didn't mean it would happen every time.

Chris's interest in Dolores was a natural development of his friendship with Esteban, spurred by his growing conviction that if he could only find out what she had done to get herself disowned, several key pieces of this worrisome puzzle would fall into place. Meanwhile, Chris wanted to know why, if there was any chance of Bertoldo's men watching the farmhouse where the secret documents were hidden, Roig had sent only Dolores to fetch them. One man with a crowbar had been no match for three with a gun. Had Roig truly underestimated his opponents that badly? And where the devil was Roig? Had he returned to Ibiza yet, or had Dolores been lying?

All at once he remembered a gravelly voice saying, "Be grateful that we were instructed not to hurt you." Involuntarily Chris stiffened in his chair. Instructed not to hurt whomever they captured? Or instructed not to hurt Chris specifically? But it was impossible! How could they have been expecting him when only Roig and Dolores knew that he might be there, unless . . . .

A chill ran up Chris's spine. Had Roig decided that he was now expendable and had set him up? And if Dolores had been part of that plan, then it was ridiculous and futile for Chris to be worrying about her safety. He was the babe in these woods, not Dolores.

A man could go paranoid. . . .

THE CHURCH in Santa Eulalia was located on the outskirts of town. A wooden building—unusual in this settlement of stucco and stone—it was small and poorly lit, and probably just adequate for year-round services in a tiny village. But on this Good Friday it was absolutely packed. Some of the older women had brought folding chairs with them to guarantee that they'd have seats. Everyone was dressed in holiday finery as Esteban had promised; the married women in long dark-colored skirts and fancy fringed shawls, the single girls in short taffeta or satin dresses and the men in black suits. Chris felt only slightly out of place in a dark brown sport coat and brown houndstooth slacks, but Esteban was impeccable in a three-piece charcoal suit that Soledad had finished pressing only minutes before they had had to leave the house.

At the end of the service, which was conducted entirely in Latin by a riveting speaker introduced as a guest celebrant, the people poured out of the church and formed a procession. They sang Latin psalms in a slow nasal manner that owed something to the earlier Moslem occupation of the island. Eight young boys, wearing white hooded robes with blue linings, carried a statue of Christ on the cross. After them came a line of girls in black dresses bearing an effigy of Our Lady of Sorrows draped in royal blue velvet. Slowly the procession climbed an uneven street lined by fourteen white stone crosses that marked the stations of Christ's travail.

There was something otherworldly about this solemn parade beneath a leaden twilight sky stabbed through at intervals by piercing shafts of lightning. Above the pilgrims loomed the fog-shrouded mountain, while below them was the rock-strewn coast besieged by angry waves. All around them a plaintive wind whistled through the sparse and twisted pines that struggled for a foothold in the inhospitable ground.

Calvary was a rocky outcropping jutting over the beach, and as the crowd of pilgrims arrived and began milling around, Chris decided to take a photograph of the young girls arriving with the likeness of the Virgin. As he searched for the best camera angle, a prosperous-looking man in a black suit appeared in his viewfinder, and Chris stiffened with surprise.

It was Roig.

Slowly the agent turned and looked at him across the clearing, and the expression in Roig's eyes was enough to turn Chris's blood to ice.

Chapter 9

"Well, Christopher, it appears that I've misjudged you," Esteban said with a smile as they walked through the front door of the house.

"Huh?"

"I had no idea a heretic like yourself could be so moved by one of our primitive spectacles. You didn't say more than five words all the way home."

Chris heard the clip-clop of the mule cart being driven away as Soledad shrugged off her beaded shawl and hurried into the kitchen to warm up their dinner.

Esteban led the way into the living room. "Shall we indulge in an apéritif?" he suggested. "Some *rumani*, perhaps, to take the chill from our bones?"

"Another native beverage?" Chris eyed the fireplace. It had turned quite cold out, and the canopy over the mule cart hadn't been much protection during the ride back to the house. As welcome as the offer of an alcoholic drink was, it probably wouldn't be as immediately satisfying as a roaring blaze in the hearth.

Chris waited until Esteban had turned and was coming toward him with a glass of amber wine in each hand. Then, pointing to the fireplace, he asked, "May I?"

"By all means," Esteban agreed. He set Chris's glass down on the raised hearth beside one of the chairs, then sank with a sigh into the other one. "So, Christopher, did our little performance truly strike you dumb this evening?"

"It was impressive," Chris conceded, "but that wasn't the reason for my preoccupation." The grate had already been set up. As he struck a long wooden match on the stone lining of the hearth, Chris explained, "I saw someone there that I wasn't expecting to run into in Santa Eulalia."

"Yes," Esteban said in a dissatisfied voice. "I saw her, too."

"Her?"

"Dolores, of course. Isn't that who you meant?"

Chris surprised him by shaking his head. "No . . . it was a man . . . in a black suit."

"I'm sure you couldn't mean Roig," Esteban said frowning.

"As a matter of fact, I do mean Roig," Chris said, as casually as he could.

"That swine," Esteban muttered vehemently. "You know him? Well, stay away from him, Christopher— he poisons everything he touches."

"Isn't that overstating the case a little?" Chris ventured, even though he was beginning to share his friend's opinion.

"I hardly think so." And the count grimly tossed down the last of his *rumani*.

Chris had taken his seat by then and sampled his

own glass of rosemary wine, which he found dry and delightfully fragrant.

"How *do* you know Roig?" Esteban demanded suddenly, and Chris was at a loss for several seconds how to answer this bald-faced question.

"I . . . met him once in Paris," he finally replied.

"He's like a python. He wraps himself around you and then he squeezes and squeezes. . . ." Esteban made a disgusted face and got up to refill his glass. "Don't let him get close to you, Christopher. The only way to escape a grasp like his is by leaving part of yourself behind. Roig isn't particular—he'll take your integrity, your honor, your self-respect . . . your will to live. . . ."

Esteban stood very still for a moment, his jaw muscles working as Chris's curious gaze rested steadily on the defeated slope of his shoulders. "He took away Diego's will to live," came a strangled voice Chris hardly recognized, "by seducing his wife."

Chris was speechless with shock. Roig, Dolores's lover? But Fernando Roig was Captain Hurteau, with a wife and two grown sons in Paris, and Dolores only worked for him. Didn't she?

Moving swiftly to the living-room door, Esteban closed it and returned to his seat facing Chris. "Christopher, I have a confession to make to you. When I was lecturing in Paris, we became friends partly because you reminded me so much of Diego. Not in appearance, of course, but in your mannerisms, your turn of phrase, your youthful energy. He had been dead for several months, and I missed him terribly. Talking to you was like having a part of him back."

"And now?" Chris asked in a thick voice.

"Now his memory has been laid to rest and you and

I are friends quite apart from it. At least, I hope we are, because I'm about to reveal something to you that only a close friend should know, and I'm relying on your discretion to keep it between us." Esteban took a deep breath before continuing, "When Diego was shot everyone assumed it was murder. The police launched an investigation, and I rushed to Barcelona to comfort the grieving widow. Only she didn't seem very grief-stricken. It wasn't until months later that I found out why. Five months after the funeral, when I had returned to Ibiza, Roig showed up at my door to offer his condolences and give me a note—Diego's suicide note."

"How kind of him," Chris remarked sarcastically.

"It said that Dolores had been unfaithful to him and that he no longer felt he could live with such a stain on his honor. He also apologized for the disgrace he was about to visit on the family by ending his miserable existence." Esteban's voice faltered toward the end, but he recovered his composure at once and went on, "Roig freely admitted that he was Dolores's lover. He also told me that he'd been the first to arrive on the scene after Diego's death, and that he'd removed the note and arranged things to look like a murder instead of a suicide before calling the police. He wanted a 'reward' for doing this, claiming he deserved one for protecting the good name of the de Charracas," Esteban said bitterly. "When I pointed out that if he'd stayed away from Diego's wife there would have been no suicide to cover up, his polite veneer came away and he gave me an ultimatum: if I refused to pay him he was going to send the note to a large Spanish newspaper and make our disgrace common knowledge."

"You didn't pay him, did you?" Chris said.

Esteban smiled thinly. "No, I managed to leap clear of the python's coils. I snatched the note from his hand, tore it into small pieces and threw them into the burning fireplace. Then I told him that if he revealed what he knew about Diego's death I would deny it, and since he was obviously such a scoundrel my word would be more readily accepted than his. Finally I ordered him out of my house, warning him never to come back. But before he left he explained why he had taken so long to bring the note to me. It seems he'd spent the intervening time attempting to blackmail Dolores with it, and when she'd finally refused to knuckle under to his demands, he'd followed through on his threat to reveal her infidelity to her father and to me. He was *smiling*, Christopher. He'd just shattered the pride of two families, destroyed a woman's reputation and caused a man's death, and he was *smiling*! Now do you see why I want you to avoid him at all costs?"

Chris was stunned. "Wait a minute," he blurted out as something occurred to him. "You destroyed the note without getting it analyzed by the police?" Esteban nodded grimly. "Then how can you be sure it was authentic?"

"It was on Diego's private stationery and I recognized my brother's handwriting," Esteban said with finality in his voice. Chris realized that there was no arguing with the count on that score.

"Poor Diego," Esteban sighed. "He was so weak. If it had been my wife I would have killed her *and* her lover without hesitation. No jury in Spain would have convicted Diego if he'd only picked up that gun to avenge his honor like the true son of a Catalan knight. Instead he put it to his own chest and pulled the trigger."

An alarm went off in Chris's mind. Suicides almost never shot themselves in the chest, he recalled reading somewhere—there was too great a risk of missing the heart and just badly wounding oneself. But that was only one of many details that didn't seem to gibe. Roig had told Chris that, while on a mission, he'd deliberately cultivated Esteban's hatred to get closer to someone else. To whom? Whose trust was worth the havoc he'd wreaked? And what could have induced Dolores to join forces with the one man she should have hated more than anyone in the world?

Esteban's explanation was raising more questions than it answered.

"What about Dolores?" Chris asked.

Esteban heaved a sigh. "I went to Barcelona and told her to pack a suitcase with all the belongings she had brought to the marriage. Then I gave her a ticket to Ibiza and informed her that the *casa* was no longer her home. Her father wanted nothing to do with her— having heard Roig's story—and I warned her to stay away from me. She must be supporting herself somehow, although I can't imagine who on the island would employ her."

At that moment there was a gentle tapping on the door, and Soledad appeared to announce that dinner was on the table.

IT HAD RAINED during the night, but the clear morning sky held the promise of a beautiful day, and despite the questions still buzzing in his head, Chris vowed to enjoy at least this one day of his vacation. At breakfast he asked the count if he could borrow a bicycle to go into Ibiza.

"I'm going to ask Colette to come riding with me today. If we end up going any distance across the island I won't be back for lunch," Chris explained happily.

On her way back to the kitchen with the dirty dishes, Soledad uttered an unimpressed "Hmph!"

But the count's eyes were full of concern as he warned quietly, "Please be careful, Christopher. I don't like Roig's suddenly turning up in Santa Eulalia. It gives me a very bad feeling."

Chris longed to be able to reassure his friend, but a sinking feeling in his stomach told him he was already caught in the python's coils.

Ibiza looked liked a carnival today, its streets filled with "free spirits" from many lands. Chris noticed a preponderance of denim-clad students with back-packs amidst the colorful crowd. Everyone seemed to have been drawn out to stroll along the Paseo Vara de Rey by the welcome warmth of the sun. He also observed a sudden crop of stars-and-stripes and maple-leaf insignias, and guessed that the North American contingent of *turistas* had arrived to do their bit for the island's economy.

Usually Chris avoided the center of town when going to Colette's hotel, but today he decided to immerse himself in humanity by taking a shortcut. From Ibiza's main street he could see Dalt Vila, or Upper Town, a charming slice of the sixteenth century with its steep stone steps and its narrow cobbled streets winding up among the dignified old *casas* that clustered in the shadow of a huge fortress.

Chris noticed a crowd gathering on a street corner. At first he thought there might have been an accident, but then he heard ripples of laughter and walked his bike closer to see what was going on.

A trio of young mimes had set up on the street, performing silent vignettes and then passing the hat among the crowd. As Chris found a spot that afforded him a good view of their act, he saw that they were portraying robots—making their limbs and bodies move in the jerky mechanical manner that seemed to have become a fad. After elaborate preparations, one of the mimes sat down on a crate and began to play "Yankee Doodle" with agonizing slowness on a clarinet. They really were talented and funny, and Chris found himself searching his pockets for loose change to drop in the hat the next time it came around.

Then he looked up and saw her standing on the other side of the improvised stage, watching the antics of the three young performers with a sad smile on her face. Suddenly everything was forgotten—Colette, the beautiful day, the search for coins in his slacks— and Chris felt himself focus entirely on Dolores.

A few minutes later she turned away, and Chris quietly followed her down a side street, waiting until they were well away from the crowded Paseo to catch up to her. "Dolores, wait!" he called in a hoarse whisper.

She started violently, whipping around with a frightened expression on her face. "You! Do you make a habit of following me around?"

"Never mind that," he told her grimly. "Where can we talk?"

After an agonized pause, she seemed to come to a decision. "My place. Come."

Dolores lived in a small house near the Portal de las Tablas. Chris watched her lift a clay flower pot to find the key that unlocked the front door; then they walked into a whitewashed living room containing only a few chairs, a broken-down sofa and a pine cupboard.

"I'm not concerned that you'll tell anyone about this place," she told him, sliding her shawl off her shoulders and dropping it over the back of one of the chairs. "I'm moving in a day or so, somewhere where no one will find me."

Chris nodded. "I don't blame you being afraid. Especially after what happened on Thursday night. I want an explanation now."

"You were captured and interrogated," she told him with surprising candor.

"W-what?" Chris was astounded.

"It takes weeks of training to develop any resistance to the kind of will-destroying drugs that are used now. If they picked you up this afternoon and questioned you again, you'd repeat this conversation to them verbatim, and not even remember doing it. You should be thankful they used drugs instead of older, more . . . painful techniques. Now go. I've told you as much as I dare."

"Oh, no, you haven't," Chris said angrily. "There's too much going on here that doesn't make sense, and, dammit, I want some answers—straight ones—and I'm not leaving till I get them! Was that business out at the farm a setup? Did Roig order you to lure me out there so I could be grabbed?"

"No. I was as surprised as you must have been, and I couldn't warn you because the moment I stepped outside someone grabbed *me*."

"Oh." Chris was disappointed. He'd been spoiling

for a fight, but Dolores had just pulled the rug out from under him. Her face, when he studied it for telltale signs of nervousness, was composed and serene—as serene as he'd seen it the second before he was attacked in the museum. Suddenly he felt uncomfortably as though he ought to be looking over his shoulder.

"What about Roig?" he persisted.

"What about him?" she rejoined, once more the wary spy.

Chris smiled crookedly. "I'm curious to know why you're working for Fernando Roig, of all people... Señora de Charraca."

She didn't look surprised. "So Esteban finally told you everything?" she murmured.

"Everything he knew... or cared to know."

"I'm sure he must have denounced me as an adulteress, and blamed me for driving Diego to suicide," she said bitterly.

"Yes, he did. Is it true?"

"No, but Esteban would never believe me," Dolores sighed. "Even though I yearned to leave Diego, while I was married to him I remained faithful."

"It... wasn't a happy marriage, then?" Chris faltered, feeling like an intruder on her unfortunate past.

"Happy? No woman could have been happy with Diego. He was selfish and demanding and lived in a fantasy world. His every whim had to be satisfied or he became abusive. And he used his brother shamelessly."

Chris was genuinely puzzled now. "I don't understand. Didn't you have a *festeig*? Didn't you select him over all the others who courted you?"

"Of course. But I didn't choose him because I loved

him. I chose him because my father told me to, even though I loved another."

"That's very sad," Chris murmured.

"Sometimes life tends to be that way," she replied stoically. "You'd better go now, and don't come looking for me again."

"The only time I ever came looking for you I ran into Roig instead. That's how this whole foul-up began," replied Chris with a touch of bitterness. Then he stepped out into the street, forcing himself not to look back as she slammed the door behind him.

COLETTE WAS STRETCHED OUT on a lounge beside the pool, turning the pages of a magazine. Chris only recognized her because of the swimsuit she was wearing—everything above her neck was concealed by her floppy straw hat, her owlish sunglasses and the magazine she was pretending to read. Sneaking up behind her chair, he suddenly leaned over its back and whispered, "Hi!"

A blond Colette whirled around, startled, then burst into smiles as she saw who it was. "The answer to my prayers!" she exclaimed with a laugh. "Have you come to take me away from this life of leisure? Maybe get me a job washing dishes in a café?"

Chris pretended great annoyance with himself. "Damn! I wish I'd thought of that! The best I could come up with was a bike hike to Charraca Bay."

"Ramón was mentioning that place," she said excitedly. "There's a ruined castle there, isn't there?"

"So I've been told. The view of the bay is also highly spoken of. Well, shall we go rent you a bike?"

"Absolutely!" All smiles, she leaped up from her

chair. "Give me five minutes to change first, though. I've got a little surprise for you."

Colette's surprise turned out to be—Colette, without any wig or makeup, and dressed in stylishly cut, soft denim trousers with matching shirt. Once more the freshly beautiful young woman he'd met on the boat, she was a treat for the eye, and Chris felt dangerously close to kissing her.

"Well, what do you think?" she asked, tossing her shiny brown hair.

"Think of what?" he replied, barely keeping a straight face.

"Men!" Colette sighed in exasperation.

"I think it's charming. You're such a lovely girl that I have to wonder why you bothered bringing that wig at all."

"It's my alter ego; the girl who goes out drinking and dancing in discos all night and just generally raising hell," she explained cheerfully. By now they had arrived at the bike rack in front of the hotel. As Chris unlocked the rear wheel of Colette's bicycle with the key the rental agent had given him, she remarked thoughtfully, "You know, I came to Ibiza with the idea of getting into all kinds of trouble, and instead here I am preparing to pedal a bike up and down hills."

"Having second thoughts?" Chris asked, straightening up and wiping his hands on his pant legs.

Without a moment's hesitation, Colette replied, "No." As their eyes met the smile they shared radiated enthusiasm and affection.

Adopting an easy pace, they set out cross-country and reached the summit of the coastal ridge in just over two hours, after stopping briefly in the town of

Balafi to buy some bread, sausage, cheese and pastries for a picnic lunch. The sky had changed gradually from blue to gray as they rode, until by the time they had coasted down to Charraca Bay it was low and threatening. The sea was the color of molten lead, its waves crashing angrily onto the rugged shore.

"I should have known it would be too good to last," Colette sighed as the first raindrops began to fall.

But Chris was undaunted. "Come on," he urged her. "Grab the food and follow me. We'll have a picnic in the dungeon."

"The dungeon?" she echoed dubiously.

"In the ruined castle. See it, right by the cliff? I happen to know that the dungeons have been restored," he told her. "Hurry, before everything gets soggy!"

It was less a castle than a tumbledown villa. They had no trouble getting inside, for the door had long since rotted off its hinges. As she gazed around at the peeling whitewash, the caved-in roof and the weeds sprouting from the earthen floor, Colette wrinkled her nose and muttered, "This is a castle?"

"When everyone else lives in one-room mud huts, yes, this is a castle," Chris told her. "Look for a trap door into the basement."

The trap door, when they found it, was so worm-eaten that it looked as though it might fall apart if they tried to lift it. Carefully Chris worked his fingers around it and levered it upward, revealing a stairway of freshly laid cement. This was the beginning of the renovated area Esteban had told him about.

Chris led the way down the stairs and into a long corridor with new brick walls. Iron doors with grill windows had been set into the walls at five-yard intervals, and from the dim light that shone through the grills on one side Chris guessed that half of the cells looked out on the bay. He opened the first door and entered an absolutely bare rectangular room with narrow slits cut out of its far wall to serve as windows.

"Would milady care to spread her picnic out here?" he asked.

"Let's see what's next door," Colette replied.

"Nothing much better, I'll bet. This is a dungeon, not a hotel," he reminded her with a smile, and began setting out the food.

"Oh, let's try one more," she insisted. "We may even find a hidden treasure." Without waiting for Chris's reply, Colette disappeared down the corridor. Her voice floated back to him. "Hey, there's a locked door here—wait a minute. A key's in the lock. . . . " A moment later he heard her scream.

"Chris!"

He launched himself into the passageway. Colette was standing in the next doorway, her face distorted with terror. She clutched convulsively at his arm when he raced up, and pointed to a corner of the cell.

A man was sprawled on the floor, making desperate efforts to stand up. In the dim light coming through the slit window Chris could make out his dark pants, checked shirt and brown hair. Despite the mud and dried blood caked on the man's face, Chris recognized him at once.

"Bertoldo!" he whispered.

Chapter 10

."Oh, my God, Chris, that's the painter!" Colette breathed in a horror-stricken voice.

Chris only nodded numbly.

"Aren't you going to do something for him?" Colette demanded. "Just look at the poor man!" Then she leaned over the prisoner and asked him something in German, to which he replied with a string of violent words that even Chris recognized as oaths and obscenities.

As Colette gasped and retreated in shock, Chris recovered his wits and told him in Spanish, "It's no use cursing her. She had no idea how she was being used."

Suddenly Bertoldo's body stiffened and he uttered another string of profanities. Colette was flabbergasted. "He speaks Spanish? But I thought—Renée said—he must have been . . . ."

"He's a spy," Chris told her flatly. "I daresay he speaks several languages. He stole important secret documents and hid them somewhere. That was why I had to use you to trap him." Then, remembering Dolores's remarks about the cruel methods sometimes used for dragging information out of people, he muttered, "In fact, he's probably been interrogated already."

Colette stared at the pathetic figure lying bound on the cold concrete floor in front of them. "Interrogated?" she cried. "It looks like torture to me! If this man stole secret documents then he should be put on trial, not locked up like an animal and mistreated." Tears stood in her eyes as she turned to confront Chris. "You can go warn whoever gives you your orders if you like, but I'm going to get a knife and cut him loose."

Chris grabbed her arm. "Wait a minute—"

"No!" she cried, and tried to shake off his hand. "I won't stand by and let a human being be treated like this!"

"I hate it just as much as you do!" Chris almost shouted. "I swear to you, Colette, I thought they'd just arrest him. If I'd known they were going to do this I would never have gone along with them. He's our enemy, but he's serving his country, and he has the right to the due process of law, just as I would if I'd been captured by his side."

Bertoldo was staring at him in disbelief. "I owe you an apology, Mr. Laval. It appears that I've misjudged you," he said in a surprisingly gentle voice. "So you and I are just soldiers doing our job. . . . I take back most of my insults, then, but I still blame you for involving the lady."

Chris kneeled beside Bertoldo, took out his Swiss Army knife and cut the rope that bound his arms and legs.

"Your trick worked beautifully, Laval," Bertoldo went on. "I really didn't think anyone was on to me. As long as I was posing as an artist I figured I couldn't refuse a commission, for fear of arousing suspicion." He opened and closed his numbed hands and massaged his rope-burned wrists with a pained sigh.

"Colette," said Chris suddenly, "we passed a small general store on our way here. Would you go get us a bottle of rubbing alcohol and some kind of gauze for applying it? Try to hide my bike when you leave, and if you see anything suspicious between here and there, just keep going and forget about us. The rain seems to have let up outside."

She nodded and disappeared into the corridor. A moment later Chris fetched part of their picnic from the next cell and watched Bertoldo wolf it down. "We can talk freely now," Chris said in a businesslike voice. "What is Roig trying to get you to tell him?"

"The name of my superior," Bertoldo replied.

Chris shook his head sadly. "I'll be honest with you—I don't like the way he's gone about this. It's unworthy of a French officer."

Bertoldo snorted with derision. "Don't make me laugh!"

"Listen, you may be used to this sort of thing but I'm not, and I'm sickened enough by it to make you an offer," Chris said. "If you'll promise not to try to escape, I'll find a way to get you out of here as soon as you're able to stand up."

Bertoldo cocked his head and frowned at him. "You realize, of course, that by setting me free you're committing treason?"

"I'd be committing a worse crime by leaving you here at Roig's mercy," Chris rejoined.

"I really believe you mean that." Bertoldo leaned back against his cell wall and remarked in bewilderment, "It's hard to imagine a man as upstanding as you working for Roig's dirty outfit."

"It's probably no dirtier than yours," Chris retorted. "You're stealing documents in France and directing them to your country, and we're taking them back and arresting you—it's all part of the game, as you'd say."

"Directing them to my country?" Bertoldo repeated slowly.

"Or selling them to the highest bidder, or whatever. Roig wouldn't give me all the details. That he's amoral and has a wide sadistic streak we both already know, but his failings don't change the basic issues."

Bertoldo's eyes were wide with astonishment. "Selling them to the highest bidder?" he echoed. "Laval, do you honestly believe that's what's going on?"

Chris shrugged. "Of course."

"Will you answer a couple of questions?" Bertoldo's voice was vibrating with tension.

"I'll try."

"When you spoke French to the girl I detected an accent, although I couldn't place it. Can you tell me your nationality?"

"I'm Canadian," Chris replied.

"That's the official story. What's your real citizenship?"

"Canadian," Chris said, puzzled. "What did you think?"

Bertoldo stared at him. "I originally thought you were a renegade, but after that tirade about our duties to our respective countries I took you for a Communist agent who had somehow become entangled in this affair."

"A-a Communist agent?" Chris was stammering in confusion. Suddenly it was crystal clear to him just how gross and appalling the deception had been. With a terrible sinking feeling in the pit of his stomach, he said faintly, "There's been a misunderstanding. . . . Look, why the devil were you following me?"

Before Bertoldo could reply, Colette rushed into the room. "There are two men on a motorcycle coming down the hill!" She gasped, leaning breathlessly against the doorjamb.

"That could be Roig," Chris remarked grimly. "We'd better move fast."

But Bertoldo was shaking his head. "Give me your knife, then both of you run for it."

"We're not leaving without you," Chris told him in a tone of voice that brooked no argument. He reached down and hauled Bertoldo to his feet. The agent's knees were a little unsteady, but he was able to stand.

"Don't be foolish, Laval," he growled. "As soon as they find my cell empty they'll start searching. I'll only slow you down. Leave me here."

"Forget it."

"How far do you think you'll get dragging me along?" Bertoldo demanded.

"I don't know," replied Chris tightly. "But we'll get a lot farther if you'll move your legs instead of your mouth."

A slow smile spread across the agent's battered face. "Okay, it's your show. Where are we going?"

"I saw stairs at the end of this corridor, going down," Chris said with sudden resolve. "There must be a sub-basement below this level, and if I remember my history correctly, there was always a lower entrance to the dungeons."

"Let's hope Roig didn't study the same history you did," said Bertoldo as they each took one of his arms and helped him along the passageway.

Sure enough, a cement stairway took them down to another corridor lined with cells. But it ended with a locked iron door.

"Damn!" Chris glanced at Colette, whose eyes were saucerlike with fear.

"We're not stopped yet," declared Bertoldo. "Give me your knife."

They looked on in astonishment as the agent fitted the corkscrew attachment of Chris's knife into the lock and jiggled it gently as he turned it to the right. The tumblers yielded with a click, and as Bertoldo pushed the door open Chris remarked, "It seems you're a man of many talents." The agent nodded and smiled. He carefully locked the door behind them.

Outside they found themselves on a rocky, crescent-shaped bit of beach perched between the relatively calm water of the bay and the sheer cliff behind them.

"We're trapped!" Colette exclaimed in a quavery voice.

"No, we're not," Chris told her, and pointed across the bay to where a concrete pier jutted into the water. On the shore nearby stood a boxlike structure without any visible windows. "I'm willing to bet there's someone tending that shed."

"It's almost a quarter-mile swim," Bertoldo warned him quietly.

But Chris was already stripping off his turtleneck, pants and shoes. "It's also our only chance," he pointed out, "and I don't think either of you could make it right now." He glanced significantly at the iron door. Roig could probably jimmy it open just as easily as Bertoldo had done. "We haven't got much time," Chris added.

"Stay underwater as much as possible," the agent advised him. "We have similar coloring, and if they're watching the water they'll probably mistake you for me and start shooting."

"All right. My story, by the way, is going to be that you fell and hurt your leg, so practice your limp while I'm gone."

The water was freezing cold. Recalling Bertoldo's warning, Chris stayed underwater as long as he could, then surfaced and turned to scan the top of the cliff before striking out across the bay. If someone was watching the water, he was doing it from inside one of the cells.

Suddenly Chris thought of the picnic they'd left on the floor of the cell next to Bertoldo's. As he stroked, Chris mentally reviewed what he'd set out for lunch, relaxing only when he'd reassured himself that nothing about the discarded picnic could possibly point to him or Colette.

His limbs were growing numb and heavy and there was a roaring in his ears, but Chris forced his arms and legs to keep moving in rhythm, counting the beats aloud when it appeared that his strength was failing him a good hundred yards from the pier. As he drew nearer he realized that there were two large dories on the other side of the pier, and that the entrance to the shed was open.

Only fifteen yards to go. Chris's whole body was numb, but he kept it moving by reminding himself that Colette was depending on him. He had to make it, for her. He couldn't, he *wouldn't* let her down! Each stroke, each kick was now a small victory of spirit over flesh as he refused to give up and drown only feet from shore.

Suddenly a searing pain shot down the back of his right leg. A cramp! There was a procedure to follow—he searched his sluggish mind and it gave him the image of a swimmer doing the jellyfish float and massaging the cramped muscle. But he felt so weary, and his arms would barely obey him as it was. . . .

"*Ayuda!* Help! *Ayudame!*" he called weakly. His eyes were trying to close. If only he could rest. . . . Then, all at once he heard a babble of voices and hands were pulling him out of the water.

"Who are you?" someone demanded.

"Are you crazy? Don't you know that it's too early to go swimming in the bay?" a second voice scolded him.

Shivering uncontrollably, Chris tried to work his lips and found that they would only move at quarter-speed, making his voice sound flat and alien. "My friend . . . hurt his leg," he managed to say. "On the beach . . . under castle . . . can't walk. Can you . . . help?" He gazed beseechingly into a thin, leathery face belonging to a man in his early fifties. As he watched, the man's expression softened, then hardened again as he clapped Chris on the back.

"You've been brave for your friend," the old fisherman told him. "Yes, we'll help. Felipe!" he called, and a third voice answered.

"Go with Claudio and 'Jandro here in one of the dories to pick up the wounded man," the fisherman continued in an authoritative voice. "And bring me your flask. This fellow's fire is nearly out."

Although without fragrance and practically devoid of taste, the fierce beverage in the small glass bottle that was now pressed to Chris's lips was incredibly reviving. By the time the dory returned across the bay, he'd regained control of his limbs and his skin had lost its bluish cast. Bundled in a thick blanket he watched as Bertoldo and Colette were assisted onto the pier.

"Chris! Are you all right?" Colette cried in French, hurrying over to him. "When they shot at you I nearly—"

"Ssh!" Chris cut her off, paling at the thought. "They might understand French."

But apparently the fishermen were blissfully unilingual, and they busied themselves with hauling the dory back up its wooden rails out of the water.

Limping dramatically, Bertoldo came over, handed Chris his clothes then satisfied Chris's curiosity in a low voice. "I was right. Roig saw you swimming and shot at you, thinking you were me. But you were out of range by then, and the bullets landed harmlessly in the water behind you. He left before the dory picked us up, but I don't think it would be wise to linger here."

Just then the old fisherman approached and asked, "Where shall we take you, *señores y señorita?*"

Chris was surprised. "You have transportation?"

"Of course." The old man was highly amused. "My son's pick-up is parked behind the shed. He'll drive you wherever you want."

Chris turned questioning eyes to Bertoldo, who replied, "Santa Eulalia. I ... know the doctor there. He's a good man, the soul of discretion."

When Alejandro had fetched the truck Chris was relieved to see that it was fitted with a closed back, increasing their chances of getting home unseen. He and Bertoldo got into the rear compartment, while

Colette rode up front with Alejandro—a tall, cheerful young man with a mass of curly black hair.

By the time the truck pulled up in front of the doctor's house in Santa Eulalia, Chris felt completely recovered from his ordeal, and he refused Bertoldo's invitation to accompany him inside and be checked over.

"What's the matter? Don't you trust me?" Bertoldo asked with a smile as Chris helped him to the doctor's door.

"Obviously I do, or else I wouldn't be leaving you here," Chris pointed out. "But I need the answers to a great many questions. Can you give them to me?"

Bertoldo shook his head regretfully. "Not without clearance. I'm sorry."

"Then get clearance. I'm sick and tired of the mushroom treatment—I've been kept in the dark and buried in fertilizer by both sides, and now I want some facts."

"I'll see what I can do. Either way you'll be contacted," the agent promised. "Until then, for God's sake, don't make a move." Waving at Colette, Bertoldo added, "I'm grateful to you. Both of you." Then he disappeared inside the house.

Chapter 11

"Some picnic *that* turned out to be," Colette sighed, and tossed a rock into the water.

After leaving Bertoldo at the doctor's house in Santa Eulalia, Alejandro had driven them back to Colette's hotel. They thanked the young man warmly then made their way down to the beach and sprawled there, exhausted. It was late afternoon by now. Most of the ill-effects of Chris's icy swim seemed to have passed, except for the occasional shudder that ran involuntarily through his body, making his teeth chatter.

"I owe you an apology, Chris," she said suddenly. "The other day, by the bridge, I didn't believe you when you told me you were just a guy who'd stumbled into a lousy situation. And I took your claim that you were an associate professor with a large grain of salt, too, even after we'd made up."

"Oh?" Chris heaved himself up on his elbows. "What convinced you I was telling the truth?"

"Some comments that Bertoldo made while you were swimming for help. He said you had a lot of guts for a civilian with no stake in the mission."

Chris sighed and turned his troubled eyes out over the rippled water of the bay. "He can't imagine what my stake is in this affair," he murmured.

"You're in trouble, aren't you?"

Chris nodded. "Not even I know how deep it is yet," he replied thoughtfully.

"Let me help you, Chris," she pleaded. "I already know something about your situation. I know that you used me to trap Bertoldo so someone named Roig could try to force information out of him, only now you're not sure whether you were working for the good guys or the bad guys. If you were working for the good guys then you're in trouble for setting him free, and if you were working for the bad guys without knowing it you're also in trouble because they could decide you know too much of the truth and try to bump you off."

"And you, too," he reminded her. "It was wrong of me to involve you, Colette. I almost wish we'd never met again on the island."

There was a pause, then she declared briskly, "Well, right or wrong, I'm in it up to my neck now, aren't I?"

Chris gazed sadly at her. "I'm afraid so," he sighed. "When is your tour supposed to be returning to France?"

"Wednesday morning. Why?"

"You're going to have to be very careful until then. Stay with the group and don't talk to anyone you don't know. Pretend not to understand Spanish if necessary. Double lock your door. Don't order anything from room service—eat in the hotel dining room where there'll be plenty of people around. And don't give your room number out to *any*one."

"You're telling me to act paranoid," she said, puzzled.

"Yes, but it can't be helped. I don't know how much Roig knows about you, and we don't want to give him any openings."

"Just a minute," she said stubbornly. "Before you draft me into this little war I have to know what it's about. Facts, please, and start at the beginning. How did *you* get involved in it?"

Her expectant gaze didn't waver from his face. After a moment's consideration, Chris decided it would be wrong to treat her as cavalierly as he'd been treated so far. Her life might be in danger, and that gave her every right to know what was going on.

He began with his first meeting with Roig in Paris and brought her up-to-date. Colette's face changed expression several times during the recitation, going from interest to shock to puzzlement to anger and back, and she stopped him at intervals to ask clarifying questions. When he was done she exhaled gustily and summed up, "Then either Roig has been manipulating you or Bertoldo is about to."

Chris nodded. He was in a double bind. If Roig was a traitor, then Chris would have to change sides at once. But if Roig was working for the French government, as he claimed, then Bertoldo, as the villain, wouldn't have thought twice about inventing a story that would raise doubts in Chris's mind about Roig's integrity. Espionage was the science of sorting out red herrings, and Chris was faced with a couple of ticklish ones. What was worse, he couldn't simply declare himself neutral at this point. He knew enough to be dangerous to both sides, and so, it occurred to him, did Colette.

Their situation got worse the more Chris thought about it, and the deepening frown on Colette's face indicated that she was having similar ideas.

"We're in a mess," he muttered disgustedly to himself. "Colette, I'm sorry I dragged you into this."

When he looked up he saw an uncertain smile on her face. "I can't think of anyone I'd rather be in a mess with. At least we're together, and we do have some hope. One of these characters has to be telling the truth, since they're obviously sworn enemies. Once we've figured out who the liar is we're home free. You didn't really mean what you said earlier, did you? About wishing we'd never met again on Ibiza?"

Chris smiled in spite of himself. "No. My happiest moments this week have been with you. If I hadn't bumped into you at that little church on the hill, my vacation would have been seven solid days of misery and confusion."

Colette drew nearer. "I'm glad you feel that way," she said shyly. "If it hadn't been for you I would probably have wasted a lot of time and energy doing the things I felt everyone *should* do on a vacation, instead of relaxing and enjoying myself."

"Relaxing!" he laughed. "If you thought this afternoon's adventure was relaxing and enjoyable, then you're better cut out for spying then I am, Miss Vaubois."

"I'm not talking about this afternoon," she protested, "although before I knew how high the stakes were I admit I was enjoying the excitement. No, I meant the walk up the ridge behind your friend's house, and on this beach that first day...." She blushed with the memory of how that stroll had nearly turned out, and noticing the sudden redness of her complexion, Chris felt his own cheeks grow warm.

"We . . . we seem to enjoy the same things," he remarked awkwardly.

Suddenly the conversation was unraveling at the seams. Colette blushed furiously and hung her head while Chris searched his mind for pleasant, noncommittal things to say to her, coming up empty each time and feeling frustrated because the one thing he longed to tell her would have bound her inextricably to the tangled mess he'd made of things. Colette didn't seem to blame him for getting her involved in his troubles, but Chris blamed himself. He'd vowed to himself that he was going to send her out of his life the moment an opportunity presented itself, and he didn't want to confuse the issue by introducing emotions.

"I think it's time I got home," he said, rising slowly to his feet and reaching for her hand to help her up. "And remember, no talking to strangers, keep your . . . door . . . locked. . . ." Colette had slid easily into his arms, and as he gazed into her large hazel eyes his thoughts evaporated, leaving him with a single desire.

Gently their lips touched, and Chris felt Colette's slender body molding against his, tender and yielding beneath the urgent pressure of his hands. The kiss deepened, became an intimate sharing, and as passion flowed like a sweet fire between them Chris felt his body responding to her with a vigor he thought had dissolved in the cold water of Charraca Bay.

For that endless moment everything was right with the world. Chris was holding a beautiful, desirable woman in his arms, and as the gate opened into a garden of delights, Roig and Bertoldo and what they stood for melted like a barely remembered nightmare into the depths of Chris's subconscious.

But then Colette murmured in a languid voice as they drew apart, "Don't talk to strangers, keep my door locked. . . . It'll be like having my mother along."

"It's only for a couple of days more," he muttered unhappily. "Come on, let's get you up to your room."

THE FOLLOWING DAY was Easter Sunday, and Chris accompanied Esteban to high mass in Santa Eulalia. As they slowly descended the church steps after the service, Chris suddenly felt himself bumped from behind, and at the same moment something was pressed into his hand.

"*Perdone*," mumbled a nondescript little man who turned his face away as he hurried past them and disappeared into the crowd.

Chris glanced quickly into the palm of his hand and saw a piece of paper, folded so many times that it formed a small cube. Not daring to entrust it to his pocket, he kept his hand closed around the message all the way back to Esteban's house. There he went immediately into his room and changed, but not before he'd opened out the note and read it: "Cemetery gate, Santa Eulalia, 3:00 p.m."

Chris felt his heart sink. The note wasn't signed. Was it from Roig or from Bertoldo's boss? Was this an invitation to have his questions answered, or a summons to death?

For more than an hour he mulled over this mysterious message, finally deciding to put in an appearance. If the meeting turned out to be with Roig, perhaps Chris could talk his way out of things, or at least postpone anything happening until he'd had a chance to seek protection from Bertoldo's side.

At three sharp, Chris arrived at the cemetery. Recalling the to-do Ramón had made about getting the key to let Colette in, Chris was surprised when the gate swung open at his touch. Hesitantly he began to walk down the main path, between rows of centuries-old tombstones that had begun to suffer from the inclement Ibizan spring weather.

Suddenly a voice behind him said cheerfully, "Right on time, Mr. Laval!" Chris whirled. There was no one in sight.

"Where are you!" Chris asked as his eyes roamed around the graveyard.

"Behind this touching monument to a dear, departed husband," came the voice.

Chris took a tentative step toward the large, ornately sculptured gravestone that hid the speaker from him.

"Stay where you are." The voice was crisp, commanding. "I can spare you only a few minutes, so I suggest you get on with the questions you were troubling a friend of mine with."

"Who are you?" Chris asked. "How do I know—"

"Come, come, Mr. Laval. Does a chilly swim and a damsel in distress mean anything to you? Now get on with it."

"All right." Chris took a deep breath. "Who are you working for?"

"Certain government agencies—I can't be more specific than that."

"And where does Roig fit in?"

"Roig's a traitor. He *was* working for the French Ministry of Defense, but now he's working for himself, buying or stealing information and selling it to the highest bidder, left or right, he doesn't care. Roig isn't his real name, by the way—it's Hurteau."

No surprise to me, thought Chris. Aloud he asked, "If you know what he's doing, why don't you arrest him?"

"Because he's on a short leash," the agent explained. "When we grab Hurteau we want to put his whole organization out of business—contacts, couriers, sources, everyone. We've had him under surveillance for some time, and he's very obligingly led us to all his associates. We're nearly ready to close him down."

"He told me Bertoldo was the agent who'd been following me."

"That's correct. We've been watching you for more than five weeks now. Somehow Roig got wind of it and was desperate to learn how much we knew about his operation. That's why Bertoldo was so important to him."

So Roig had suspected that time was running out, Chris mused. *No wonder he was suspicious of me when I met him by accident that first day, asking me who had told me of his whereabouts. He must have known Bertoldo could not have been far away, and he couldn't have been sure I hadn't somehow been drafted to the other side.*

The cold voice cut into his thoughts. "Are there any more questions?"

"Yes," Chris replied, with more confidence than he felt. "Why was I being followed in the first place?"

"Hurteau has a pipeline to the Ministry files. You apparently agreed to carry messages for him back to Canada when you went home this summer. Roig has been attempting to expand his operations there. We intercepted and decoded the letter he sent to his contact in Montreal, advising him that you would be bringing over some vital information he hoped to have by summer. After that it was standard procedure to keep an eye on you. When we interrogated you and discovered how little you knew, the surveillance was discontinued."

"The interrogation—was that out at the old farmhouse?"

"Yes. You swing a mean crowbar, by the way. Put one of our men out of action for two days."

Chris grinned involuntarily at this left-handed compliment, but there was something nagging at the back of his mind, something he had to clear up. "What about the art theft? Roig's agent, a woman named Dolores, was involved."

Roig dealt in intelligence, and if Roig had staged the theft at the *casa* it meant that Esteban or one of his staff was also dealing in intelligence. Why else would Dolores have been tearing picture frames apart?

"I don't know anything about that," the voice said casually, but Chris thought he detected a new note of reserve.

"I think you do and you don't want to tell me," Chris contradicted him in a quiet voice. "In fact, the more I think about it, the less sense it makes that Dolores de Charraca should be working for the man who ruined her reputation. She comes from an old-fashioned Ibizan family, and she'd be far likelier to avenge herself on Roig than help advance his schemes. Don't you agree?" There was no reply, and Chris continued. "I think she's a double agent, working with you to destroy Roig. Am I right?"

"You'll have to ask Señora de Charraca about that.'

I can't tell you anything." The voice sounded impatient.

Chris heaved a sigh. "You can't and she won't."

"Well, if that takes care of your questions—"

"Not quite," Chris interrupted. "I still have to make up my mind which side is telling the truth, but if I go with your side, how can I contact you to let you know of any developments?"

The voice was silent for a moment. "There's a drop you can use, since you already know about it. It's the doctor's house where you left Bertoldo yesterday. Put your message in an envelope and seal it, then write 'Gacetillero,' on the outside and slip it through the doctor's mail slot. Now, you leave first . . . and don't look back."

As Chris strolled toward the gate, he muttered the name over and over to himself—"Gacetillero." It meant reporter in Spanish. Where had he seen it used as a name before?

Eva Tirso's address book! The one he'd been looking at when she caught him in her office and flew into such a rage. Suddenly he thought he understood why Eva had behaved so on edge with him. . . .

ESTEBAN WAS SITTING in the living room with a glass of wine and a historical journal when Chris returned to the house late that afternoon. After his discussion with "Gacetillero" Chris had gone for a little walk to verify something he'd suspected all along—the doctor's house was only a block and a half from the post office. That meant that Eva could have been making "drops" every time she came into town to mail a letter, although it didn't prove anything conclusively. If he could only get into her desk and look for that address book. . . . Bertoldo's name appearing among the Bs would be tremendously enlightening.

The next day Esteban greeted Chris at breakfast with the news that he had been to early mass and intended to spend the morning out at the dig. He invited Chris along, but the offer was politely declined. Chris had other plans for his morning, plans he'd rather no one saw him carry out.

When Soledad was busy cleaning the kitchen floor, he quietly entered the office, closing the door after him. Then he tried the drawers of Eva's desk. They were locked, of course. What had he expected?

Suddenly he remembered how Bertoldo had used the corkscrew attachment of his knife two days earlier. Basic honesty made him hesitate. But then he decided that after all he'd been through he was entitled to think of himself as a spy, and he pulled out the corkscrew and inserted its point gingerly into the lock. After considerable jiggling, the gadget found the tumblers and Chris was able to slide the middle drawer open.

To his disappointment it contained only a cassette tape recorder. But just as he flexed his fingers to close the drawer again he heard a muted click, and watched in amazement as the wheels inside the cassette began to turn. A few seconds later they stopped again. What the devil was going on?

Gently he ran his fingers down the sides of the recorder until he'd located the plug in the microphone socket. Chris pulled it out and placed it on the top of the desk. Then he pressed rewind and play, keeping the volume very low.

All he heard was the sound of a woman humming to herself. After a moment he recognized Soledad's voice, and that was when it struck him exactly what this device was—a voice-activated tape recorder. Eva had the count's house bugged!

With mounting excitement, Chris replaced the microphone plug in the side of the machine, then located the cable's exit hole behind one leg of Eva's desk. He followed it under the area carpet—the only one in the house—to the wall, where it had been tucked behind the telephone wire and proceeded to accompany it along baseboards and around doors to the main phone outlet in the living room. Stuck to the bottom of the telephone Chris found the coin-sized, wafer-shaped microphone.

That settled it. Eva was an agent. And the fact that she had had "Gacetillero" in her address book was a strong argument for putting her in Bertoldo's camp. Mixed with the letters in her manila envelope there had probably been a cassette or two, destined for the drop at the doctor's house. It was very interesting to know, Chris mused grimly. Very interesting indeed.

Chapter 12

Doggedly Chris trudged up the side of the ridge behind the house, picking his footing carefully on the sloping path of gravel and sand that he'd negotiated with Colette on Good Friday. This early in the morning the air was cool and refreshing, and Chris reflected that it was just what he needed to clear his troubled mind.

So Eva was a spy? That explained her rigid reserve, which Chris had originally taken for the prim modesty of a well-bred Ibizan girl. It also explained her flare of rage when she'd found him reading her address book, and the fright in her eyes when the half-empty tube of oil paint had fallen out of his jacket pocket. She'd probably received word just before lunch that Bertoldo had disappeared, and it was likely a habit among the artists in the colony to mark their paint tubes in some way to show whose they were. Small wonder he'd been lured away and interrogated that same night!

Arriving at the spot where he and Colette had rested while climbing the ridge before, Chris leaned wearily against the fallen log and let his thoughts churn freely.

So Eva was a spy. . . . Her reason for coming in on Good Friday had probably had something to do with the cassette recorder, he reasoned, setting it up to operate automatically during her absence. But that begged a very disturbing question: why was Esteban under surveillance? The count had told Chris that Eva had been his secretary for a year. They'd been watching him for a very long time! And "Gacetillero" had evaded Chris's question about the art theft Roig had staged at the *casa*. Was that because Esteban was suspected of dealing with Roig? But how *could* he be, after the conversation with Chris that Eva had undoubtedly taped concerning Roig's despicable contribution to the de Charracas' tragedy? No, there must be some other reason. A year ago. . . . The only thing Chris could think of that had happened to Esteban around that time was the death of his brother, Diego.

Chris sighed sadly and shifted position on the fallen log. He'd barely scratched the surface of this complicated mystery. He still didn't know how Dolores de Charraca fitted into the picture, or even whose side she was on. She could be working independently to exact her personal revenge, without giving a damn about politics or the law. Perhaps she *was* playing both ends against the middle. Had she latched onto the strange circumstances of her husband's death, he wondered. And how had she managed to convince Roig to trust her as an accomplice after his attempt to blackmail her had given her reason to hate him?

Good Lord! I've already cast Roig as the villain! But how else to explain his treatment of Bertoldo, and the attitude that Esteban had described encountering when Roig had visited the house? For that matter, what sense did it make for a buyer and seller of government secrets to get involved with a selfish idealist like Diego de Charraca? And what happened to all the money Diego had raised by selling the de Charraca treasures?

There was one person who could answer some of his questions—Dolores. She might not be where he'd last seen her, but Chris had no where else to start looking for her. If he found her, and if she answered his questions as directly as he hoped, his quandary would be over.

Chris hurried back down the hillside and strode boldly into the office to call a taxi.

THE KEY WAS MISSING from its hiding place under the clay pot beside Dolores's door, and Chris took that as a good sign. At first there was no answer to his knock. Then he thought he heard someone moving around inside and began to pound a little harder.

All at once he sensed that he was being watched. He whipped around and discovered a wizened old woman standing in the doorway opposite. "She's moved," the woman volunteered. "She took her things out yesterday."

"Has someone else moved in?" Chris asked.

The woman pursed her thin lips and shook her head. She opened her mouth to reply but was cut off by the crash of something falling inside the house. Chris hesitated only an instant before digging his knife out of his pants pocket and opening the corkscrew attachment. But the thought of picking the lock in front of a witness made him nervous, so he explained over his shoulder, "I think she's in there. She may be hurt or sick."

This corkscrew was coming in very handy lately, he mused as he fitted it into the lock and began to jiggle it around. And Chris's skill with it was improving— scant seconds later he was through the door.

"Dolores?" he called.

There was a faint moan from the next room.

That was where he found her. She was lying on the floor, her breath coming in sobs, and she had a large bruise on her cheek and an oozing cut in her lower lip.

"Oh, my God," he breathed.

Thrusting aside the small table that she had apparently overturned to draw his attention, Chris knelt and gently gathered her up. At the touch of his hand she began to shudder violently, and he had to hold her tightly and reassure her over and over again to calm her down. Several minutes later, when her sobs had subsided and her convulsive grip on his shirt had relaxed, he murmured softly, "Who did this to you, Dolores?"

Painfully she whispered, "Roig."

Chris's face was grim as he laid her down gently on the couch and went to fetch a rag and some water from the kitchen. Carefully he bathed her bruises, then brought her some cool water in a glass. Dolores drank painfully but eagerly. When she lay back with a sigh, Chris said quietly, "Did Roig find out that you were working for the government?"

Suddenly rigid, she gazed wide-eyed into his face and blurted out, "How . . . . Who told you?"

"I guessed."

A pause, then she remarked quietly, "You're a good guesser."

"I've had to be—nobody seems to want to tell me anything," he pointed out. "I've come to some conclusions, and I need you to tell me whether they're right. Will you do that? You won't have told me anything—I worked it all out on my own," he hastened to assure her.

Reluctantly she nodded.

"I think Diego gave Roig huge sums of money. I think the first instalment was to finance Roig's traffic in stolen documents and the subsequent instalments were to keep him quiet about the first one. Am I right?"

Dolores's dark eyes were troubled. "Partly right," she told him. "Diego did give him a great deal of money, but it wasn't for espionage activities. My husband was too much of a dreamer to accept ugly political realities," she added, and suddenly the whole story poured out of her in a bitter flood. "When Roig came to him promising to make him the ruler of Ibiza, Diego leaped at the chance. Roig convinced him that all they had to do was foment a revolution on the island and sever all ties with Spain. It was a hopeless cause, but Diego couldn't see that. He poured a fortune into Roig's scheme—or should I say Roig's pocket? He was even planning to rebuild the ruined castle on Charraca Bay and run the government from there, for once Ibiza had declared its independence who would dare oppose the sovereignty of a de Charraca, the traditional lord of the island?

"Diego took for granted that he would rule, since his brother wasn't the least bit interested in anything but his digs." Dolores gulped and averted her eyes before continuing, "Time had been considerably less kind to my family than to the de Charracas, and when Diego promised my father a position of great power in the new government in exchange for my hand in marriage, I was ordered to reject the man I loved and accept his younger brother's suit instead."

For a moment Chris was speechless. Of course, how had he missed it! No wonder Esteban had been so hard on Dolores, and so regretful in his retelling of the incident!

Suddenly plunged into confusion, Dolores stammered, "I . . . I shouldn't have told you all that. . . . "

"Yes, you should," Chris countered hastily. "And if you still have any feelings for Esteban you should tell him, too. Don't let Roig keep you apart any longer."

There was a hopeful gleam in Dolores's eye. "You mean Esteban still . . . ?"

"He's a proud man," Chris cautioned her, "and you'll probably have to do some fast talking to get him to forget the accusations against you in that alleged suicide note that Roig brought him, but—"

"What!" she exclaimed angrily. "*Roig* brought him that note?"

A terrible suspicion that had lain dormant in Chris's mind sprang to life. "Yes," he replied slowly. "He told Esteban he'd tried to blackmail you with it but you'd refused."

"He was lying," Dolores said, her dark eyes flashing with fury. "I never saw that note. The first I heard of it was when Roig told me that a counterrevolutionary group on Ibiza had decided to discredit the de Charracas by making it appear that I was an adulteress and that Diego had committed suicide. He said *they* had sent the note to Esteban."

"Then you knew it was murder all along?" Chris prompted her.

"Of course! That was why I joined up with Roig in the first place. He was going to help me uncover the murderer, since after several months of investigation, the police were apparently at a loss. I may not have loved Diego, but I was still a de Charraca."

"But then you discovered what Roig really did for a living. . . ?"

"Yes, and I contacted the French government. I never knew that Roig was behind the note," Dolores concluded tersely.

That seemed to close their discussion, but Chris could guess the rest: the ploy with the suicide note had probably been intended to force Dolores into his organization by eliminating her other options. As Esteban had told Chris earlier, neither he nor her father now wanted anything to do with her, and the circumstances of her disgrace and disownment were such that not even the local gossips cared to discuss them, as Chris had seen for himself. Add to that the fact that Diego had left her nothing to speak of—having handed over the entire family fortune to Roig before his murder—Roig must have been confident that Dolores had had no choice but to stay in his operation, even when she found out that he was a criminal.

"Mr. Laval, you have to leave," Dolores said urgently. "If Roig ever discovers how much you know you're as good as dead."

"And what about you?" he rejoined.

"You've seen a sample of what he can do when he's only annoyed," she said, touching her puffed lip. "If he ever suspects I've double-crossed him . . . ."

"That does it," Chris declared. "We're both getting out of here. Can you stand?" Shrugging off a strange feeling of *déjà vu*, he helped Dolores to her feet and made certain her legs would support her. "We're not far from the taxi stand at the Roman gate," he told her. "If you can walk with me that far, I have a plan to get you to a safe place. Will you trust me?"

Hesitating only a moment, Dolores said firmly, "Just tell me what to do."

Chris's plan was simplicity itself. Once they'd reached the taxi stand and selected a vehicle, Chris had the driver cruise past the corner where the bus to Santa Eulalia took on passengers. Leaning out the window, he called, "Who wants a free ride to Santa Eulalia?" and within seconds there were three more people in the car, two of them women. En route to the village, he proceeded to acquire for Dolores, by purchase or barter, some of the accessories the other two woman were wearing, while she changed her hairstyle at his suggestion. The other passengers were a little taken aback at Chris's impromptu auction, and he knew that word of the strange taxi ride would travel quickly around Santa Eulalia. He only hoped that Roig wouldn't hear about it until Dolores was safely out of his reach.

By the time the cab came to a halt in front of the bus station in Santa Eulalia, Dolores was wearing a printed scarf over her hair, a striped woolen shawl and a wide leather belt. She'd rolled up her long black skirt at the waist, making it knee-length. Chris leaned over and murmured, "Do you know the way to the doctor's house from here?"

Her split lip prevented her from smiling, but her eyes lit up with comprehension. "Of course, it's only a couple of blocks," she whispered back. "Aren't you coming with me?"

"No. As a precaution in case we've been followed, I'm simply going to head up to the house. If everyone in the cab scatters then Roig's man will have a tough time deciding who's who, and that increases your chances of arriving at the doctor's place unseen."

The other passengers were engaged in an animated conversation and barely noticed this exchange, and it wasn't until the taxi driver announced that they'd arrived in Santa Eulalia that they showed any further interest in their eccentric benefactors. As each of them got out of the cab, he or she thanked Chris and shook his hand, but none with the emphatic gratitude that Dolores displayed.

As Esteban's house came in sight, Chris glanced at his watch and noticed with some surprise that it wasn't even noon yet. Lord! At this rate he'd need a vacation from his vacation.

Chris was reaching for the doorknob when he thought he heard his name being called. Looking around curiously, he saw Jondalitx summoning him from the side of the house. Chris's stomach began to churn. Roig couldn't have found out *already*! Reluctantly he joined the foreman near the shed.

"I'm sorry to trouble you, Mr. Laval, but I thought you should know that my friend was able to get you that plane reservation after all," Jondalitx told him in a soft voice.

"What? I nev—"

"The ticket will be waiting for you at the departures counter of the airport outside Ibiza," the agent continued, ignoring the interruption. "You're on the one-thirty flight to Palma this afternoon."

Chris took a steadying breath before asking, "And why am I going to Palma?"

Jondalitx grinned unpleasantly at him. "Why does anyone go to Palma? Whatever else you do there before coming back, give this to my good friend Hutin at the Palma airport. He's a mechanic with Air France." And the foreman slipped something small and solid into Chris's pocket. "Don't wait too long, though," he added. "Hutin has a seat on the four-twenty flight to Paris."

Gulping hard, Chris remarked in what he hoped was a casual voice, "I wasn't expecting to leave this early. Now it seems I won't be able to have lunch with Esteban. I'll just leave him a note and go immediately to the airport."

"As you wish," Jondalitx agreed. He bobbed his head a couple of times and disappeared around the side of the shed.

Chris's heart was hammering as he opened the front door and headed for his room. He'd hoped to avoid any more of Roig's "assignments," at least until his vacation was over and he could go home. But now Roig was forcing the issue, and there was no way for Chris to refuse him without arousing his suspicions. Uneasily Chris reached into his pants pocket and took out the object Jondalitx had given him. It was a metal film cannister.

What a dilemma! Chris couldn't keep the film, but he couldn't pass it on, either. Then, all at once he had an idea. It was time he let "Gacetillero" know where he stood anyway. . . .

In the office Chris found writing paper and plain envelopes in one of Esteban's desk drawers. First he scribbled a note to the count, telling him he had to go to Palma on an urgent matter and asking him to inform Colette of his whereabouts. Then he folded the page, put it into an envelope and sealed it. Next, he composed a second message containing all the information Jondalitx had given him, added a postscript explaining his plan, and placed the letter in a second envelope, which he stuffed into an inside pocket of his denim jacket. Leaving the note to Esteban sitting on the dining-room table, Chris borrowed a bicycle from the shed and set off down the road to Santa Eulalia.

At the drugstore in the village Chris purchased a roll of the same brand of film as Jondalitx had given him, sealing the foreman's cannister into the envelope destined for "Gacetillero" while the clerk was busy serving another customer. Then he raced on his bicycle over to the doctor's house and made his second "drop" of the day.

The timing was going to be very close, Chris realized as he glanced at his watch. If he rode full tilt and bypassed Ibiza proper, he still might not make his flight. Then he noticed a familiar-looking taxi parked across the road. The driver was sitting behind the wheel, munching lazily on a sandwich. Turning at the sound of hurried footsteps he recognized Chris and stepped out of his cab to greet him.

"Ah, *señor!*" the driver exclaimed happily. "What luck it was that you picked me this morning. *Five* fares to Santa Eulalia! I won't have to work hard all afternoon."

Chris waved aside the man's gratitude. "How would you like to make that much money again, right now?"

"What a question!" laughed the driver.

"All right—get me to the airport in time to catch a one-thirty flight and that's what I'll pay you," Chris told him.

"And your bicycle, *señor*?"

After only a moment's hesitation, Chris declared, "It goes, too," and tossed it in the backseat.

Chuckling delightedly, the driver started his engine.

They arrived at the airport with ten minutes to spare. After giving the driver instructions regarding the bicycle, Chris darted into the tiny terminal, claimed his boarding pass from the uniformed employee behind the departures desk and sprinted outside again to the only aircraft visible on the tarmac. It was a twin-engine propellor plane. It held eight passengers and Chris was evidently the last to board, for as soon as he had fastened his seatbelt the pilot announced that they were about to take off.

Glancing around at the assortment of people traveling with him, Chris saw a businessman with a briefcase, a couple of students in jeans and T-shirts, a pair of well-dressed women who, he gathered from their conversation, were going to Palma to shop, and a young mother with a two-year-old on her lap. Immediately behind him sat an elderly man who smiled a great deal. Apparently there was a small amount of regular traffic between Ibiza and Palma, the capital city of the next island in the Balearic chain.

As the motors of the little plane roared to life, the frightened toddler began to scream, and his high-pitched shrieks filled the cabin as they taxied to the head of the runway. As though in competition with him, the pilot revved the engines to build power for take-off. Then, suddenly both engines cut out. The propellors slowed and stopped, and a red truck with a revolving red light on its roof was racing across the tarmac toward them. A moment later the pilot turned to face his passengers. Although he spoke with professional composure, he was obviously shaken.

"Ladies and gentlemen, we're having mechanical difficulties. The emergency truck is going to tow us back to the terminal, where I'll have to ask you to disembark and board another aircraft. I'm sorry that you'll be inconvenienced, but the other plane is already being fueled, and the delay should be minimal."

"But I have a meeting in Palma in an hour!" exclaimed the businessman.

"You'll probably still make it, sir," the pilot said with a faint smile. "Or you'll be only a few minutes late."

Barely satisfied by this response, the businessman subsided into angry mutterings as the plane was towed slowly away from the runway. Finally it came to a stop and the passengers filed off.

As Chris descended the ramp he suddenly realized that an inordinate number of airport personnel were gathering at the gate. A ground hostess with a fixed smile stood at the foot of the ramp, urging the deplaning passengers to move clear of the aircraft. The pilot and copilot were the last to emerge. As they hurried down the ramp an indignant mechanic in a brown jumpsuit rushed over and engaged the pilot in a heated debate, which ended when the pilot categorically ordered the plane to be towed to the workshop.

Something about the strained faces peering out the terminal door caused a horrible suspicion to grow in Chris's mind and his heart began to pound. He searched the crowd for someone who looked authoritative, and when a middle-aged man wearing a gray blazer and a concerned scowl walked past, Chris stepped in front of him and asked in a low voice, "Was the plane sabotaged?"

Suddenly the man was all jovial smiles. "What? Of course not!" he declared emphatically. "Just a simple mechanical failure causing a loss of engine power."

Indicating the anxious crowd at the gate, Chris inquired, "And does the whole airport usually turn out to stare at a plane that's had a simple mechanical failure? Does the mechanic argue about whether it ought to go into the workshop?" Something else occurred to him and he added, "In order for that emergency truck to reach us as quickly as it did, the captain would have had to radio in about the malfunction before he even had a chance to find any!"

The man looked very uncomfortable for a moment. Finally he said, "You'll have to promise to keep this to yourself. We got a phone call telling us there was a bomb planted on the plane."

"Do you know who called?" Chris asked, although he already knew what the reply would be.

"No, it was an anonymous call—probably from Ibiza."

Chapter 13

When Chris finally arrived at Palma, he was not surprised to find out that there was no Air France mechanic named Hutin working at the Palma airport. Chris thanked the helpful clerk in the personnel department and forced himself to leave her office with a smile on his face, despite the darkness of his thoughts.

Once again he heard Dolores's warning: "If Roig ever finds out how much you know, you're as good as dead." Roig knew. That was why he'd sent Chris on this fool's errand. The cannister of film had been a red herring—the true purpose of the "mission" had been to get him on the fatal flight. It hadn't mattered that innocent people would also have been killed. Chris shivered.

But Roig had been foiled. How? Had "Gacetillero" received his message in time and somehow deduced that Chris was heading into a trap? Or had Spanish Intelligence learned about the bomb from some other source? However it had happened, Chris had escaped the fate Roig had planned for him. On his return to Santa Eulalia he would have to drop a thank-you note at the doctor's house.

Chris was tempted to spend some time in Palma, but it suddenly occurred to him that if Roig knew enough about him to want him dead, then Colette was probably also in danger. Even if she followed Chris's advice and took precautions, which was unlikely considering how headstrong she could be, she was still so vulnerable!

He caught the next flight back to Ibiza. As he disembarked from the plane, a woman with short dark hair was waiting for him at the gate.

"Mr. Laval?" she called out, her professional smile never faltering.

Frowning, he replied, "Yes, that's me."

"I have an urgent message for you. A Miss Vaubois called about half an hour ago, asking that you call her back right away. Here's the number."

Alarms were going off in Chris's head as he took the slip of paper from her hand and thanked her. There was a pay phone inside the terminal, and he wasted no time getting to it. As he fumbled for coins in his pockets, all sorts of dire possibilities were going through his mind, but they were dispelled when she answered the phone on the second ring, even though her voice trembled with fear as she said hello. At least she was alive, he thought. At least he wasn't too late.

"Hello, Colette?"

"Oh, Chris!" He could hear the tears in her voice.

"It's all right, darling." She must have heard about the bomb scare.

"I'm so frightened," she sobbed.

"I'm okay, honey. Just hang on and I'll come straight to the hotel to get you."

"No, not the hotel. I . . . I think they're watching it."

"Then tell me where to meet you."

There was a pause, then Colette blurted out as though in pain, "The dig. Where your friend Esteban is excavating, near . . . near Cala Llonga. I'm not far from there now. . . . Oh, Chris!" she wailed.

"It's going to be all right, sweetheart," he assured her. "I'll be there as soon as I can."

The bicycle was waiting for him where he'd told the cab driver to leave it, in a bike rack beside the airport parking lot. Pedaling at full speed, Chris reached the taxi stand near the Roman gate in less than fifteen minutes. The welcoming shout that greeted him as he pulled up told him that "his" driver was available, and Chris walked the bike directly to the cab and said, "I have to get somewhere fast."

"Will you pay me like before?"

"Of course."

"Then name your destination, *señor*."

"Take me to Cala Llonga," said Chris as he stowed his bike in the backseat.

Suddenly the driver looked dubious. "Those are bad roads. Pretty country but mean, narrow roads. You'd be better off on a mule."

"Then take me as close as you can," Chris sighed, "and I'll bike the rest of the way."

"*Sí, señor!*"

The taxi driver was able to take Chris closer to the dig than either of them expected. They were halfway up the ridge when he finally brought the old car to a halt. "There's a hairpin turn up ahead," he apologized.

"It sounds to me as though you've tried this once before," remarked Chris as he took out his wallet to pay the fare.

The driver only grinned. He was a large, bulky man with the shoulders of a weightlifter and the face of a boxer. "Why are you in such a hurry to get to the top of this road?" he asked.

"A friend of mine might be in trouble up there." Chris pressed several bills into the cab driver's hand and quickly got his bike out of the backseat. Just before the turn he happened to glance back. The driver was standing beside his taxi, gazing after him and slowly shaking his head.

The dig appeared to be deserted. Carefully Chris concealed his bike behind a large fallen rock, then he approached the opening of the excavation, calling softly, "Colette? It's me."

Silence. Chris was perplexed. She knew he was coming. After all, she'd chosen this spot herself. He called a little more loudly, "Don't be afraid, Colette. I'm alone."

"I'm very pleased to hear that, Mr. Laval." Suddenly Jondalitx was standing in the excavation entrance, pointing a large pistol at Chris's chest.

"Where's Colette?" Chris demanded.

"Miss Vaubois regrets that she is unable to meet you today," replied the foreman with a leer.

Chris felt helpless rage boiling up inside him. Roig must have grabbed her when she left the hotel, then forced this location out of her by his usual filthy methods...!

"Where is she, dammit?" he roared.

Jondalitx traced a lazy figure eight in the air with the gun barrel, swinging it from Chris's chest to his stomach and back, before replying insolently, "She's safe—for the moment. Did you have a pleasant flight to Palma?"

"It was delightful," Chris said tightly, trying to get a grip on himself. "I gather they found your bomb?"

"Bomb?" the foreman laughed. "Oh, we weren't as crude as that. We just bribed a mechanic to loosen a couple of bolts in one of the engine mounts. The result would have been the same."

Chris nodded grimly. "I see. Very clever." Then, indicating the weapon in Jondalitx's hand, "And now that subtlety has failed, you've decided to simply shoot me, is that it?"

If Chris had been any less angry, he would have been paralyzed with fear. But the terrible wrath that now seized him had cleared his mind, steadied his hands and sharpened his reflexes.

Suddenly aware that the gun he was holding was all that prevented Chris from tearing him apart, the foreman tightened his grip on it. He abandoned his bantering tone and said unpleasantly, "I'd like very much to shoot you, Laval. You've caused us a great deal of trouble, and you seem to be incredibly lucky. But Roig has given me other orders."

Jondalitx stepped out of the entrance and circled Chris. "Get inside," he snapped, waving the gun for emphasis.

Chris stood his ground. Glaring at his captor he said with quiet menace, "Not until you've told me where Colette is."

"She's with Roig. That's all you need to know. Now move!"

For a split second Chris debated with himself. Jondalitx obviously meant to do away with him inside the dig. Would Chris have a better chance of disarming him in the dark passageway, where he might be expecting some kind of resistance, or out here in the light? Mentally gauging the distance between himself and the gun, Chris decided he had to draw Jondalitx closer in order for his plan to succeed.

His shoulders slumped in apparent resignation, Chris turned as though to enter the dig. Three steps and he was beside the rock wall. Counting Jondalitx's approaching footsteps, he hesitated until the foreman was only a couple of yards away.

"I said move—" Jondalitx never got to finish his sentence. Pushing off from the wall, Chris launched himself like a human missile at the gun in the foreman's hand, knocking him over and grappling with him on the hard ground. When they stopped rolling Chris was on top, struggling to loosen the Ibizan's grip on the pistol as Jondalitx clawed at his face with his free hand.

Chris was tall and lanky, but Jondalitx was a manual laborer in peak physical condition, and that gave him the advantage. All at once the world turned over and Jondalitx was sitting on Chris's chest, still holding tightly to the gun and now trying to aim it downward. Despite the adrenalin surging through his body and thoughts of Colette that increased his determination to survive, Chris could feel himself losing ground. He was being forced to push upward against a weight that surpassed his own.

And then suddenly Jondalitx gave a startled yelp and seemed to fly backward. The next instant he was grappling with a more equally matched opponent—Chris's taxi driver. The driver had grabbed him from behind and now had one beefy arm around the foreman's throat, while with his other hand he twisted Jondalitx's gun arm behind his back. In a matter of seconds the weapon dropped to the ground, along with Jondalitx's limp body.

"I hope that isn't your friend," the driver said with a grin as Chris got painfully to his feet.

"Lord, no!" he replied. "If you hadn't stopped him he would have killed me." Then curiosity overcame Chris's gratitude and he asked, "What made you decide to follow me?"

"You said your friend might be in trouble. If you'll pardon me for saying this, *señor*, you may be tall but I have a twelve-year-old son I think could beat you in a street fight. A man like you should always have a man like me behind him when he goes to meet trouble. Besides," he added with a laugh, "I wouldn't let anything happen to a big tipper like you."

CHRIS STOOD OUTSIDE Eva's front door for a few moments, fingering the gun he'd taken from Jondalitx. The taxi driver was on his way into Santa Eulalia to make Chris's third "drop" of the day, with instructions to tell the doctor that the patient was to be examined by a specialist, one Dr. Gacetillero. As Chris felt the corrugated pattern of the pistol grip, his knees grew weak with the realization that he'd had two very narrow scrapes with death that day, and that he was still alive only because someone had come to his aid both times. Would Bertoldo's people now come to Colette's aid, he wondered, or did her fate rest entirely in his own two unsteady hands?

It was getting late and daylight was beginning to wane. Whatever happened now would have to happen quickly before it got too dark—for Chris had problems enough. Stuffing the gun into his jacket pocket, Chris rapped impatiently at the door. He was so tense that he started when it opened.

Eva didn't look at all surprised to see him. "Hello, Mr. Laval. You have a good memory," she greeted him. "I only mentioned my address to you once, in casual conversation, and here you are."

When she made no move to invite him in, Chris said abruptly, "I need your help. Can we talk inside?"

"I'm afraid that wouldn't be proper," she demurred with a disapproving frown.

"All right, then." His voice was low and urgent. "I know about the tape recorder in your desk and the 'drop' near the post office where you leave the cassettes. You nearly had a kitten when that paint tube fell out of my pocket the other day, so I figure you must be on Bertoldo's side, but the fact is that I don't really care. Roig has Colette Vaubois and probably intends to kill her. So whether you're with Roig or against him, the gun in my pocket says you're going to help me find him and get her back."

Eva eyed the bulge in Chris's jacket, then said quietly, "Won't you come in, Mr. Laval?"

Eva Tirso's furnishings weren't many, but they were simple and comfortable. Waving him toward an L-shaped white leather couch, she said, "Shall we forego the amenities and get right down to business?"

He nodded.

"You're right. Bertoldo and I are on the same side," she told him. "May I see the gun?"

"Why?"

She smiled thinly. "Among other things, to verify that you have one."

That sounded fair to Chris. As he drew the weapon

out of his jacket pocket for a moment to show her, he said, "I got it from Roig's man, Jondalitx. He tried to kill me half an hour ago, up at the dig."

"Is he dead?"

Chris shook his head. "Just hurt. 'Dr.' Gacetillero is probably "examining" him right now."

"I wouldn't be surprised," she commented tranquilly. "He works very fast—fortunately for you."

"Then that anonymous phone call to the airport ... ?"

" . . . came from us, yes," she supplied.

"But there was no bomb.".

"That doesn't matter. Can you think of a quicker way to ground an airplane?"

Suddenly it occurred to him why the mechanic had been so argumentative. If Chris had taken money to botch a job, the last thing he'd want would be a couple of inspectors going over it with a fine-toothed comb. But it was time to get this discussion back on the rails. "What about Roig?" he asked tersely.

"We've been watching him, but I'll have to call headquarters to find out where he is right now. Come."

She got briskly to her feet and headed for the front door. At the sound of Chris's startled cry she turned and explained patiently, "I have no telephone, Mr. Laval. On an island where there are so few, calls are too easily traced. So I use Count de Charraca's phone during the day, and the pay phone near the drugstore at night." She consulted her wristwatch. "It's still early enough, I think, and we're closer to the count's house than to Santa Eulalia. Shall we go?"

Chris jumped up and followed her out the door.

NOBODY SAW THEM ENTER. He and Eva went directly to the office where she made him turn his back while she dialed. After a pause, she spoke in a low voice into the receiver. "This is Eva. I want the surveillance report on Fernando Roig, please."

While she waited for the information, Chris paced impatiently, finally opening the door just a crack and peering into the hall. He heard Esteban's voice from the living room, asking Soledad to get him some coffee and sandwiches.

"Yes, that's right—Fernando Roig," Eva was repeating a little more sharply into the telephone. "Shall I spell it for you?"

Suddenly there was a commotion going on outside.

"What are you doing here?" Esteban bellowed angrily.

Dolores's voice declared, "You're going to listen to me! Before I die you're going to know the truth!"

Good girl, Chris thought, an instant before Eva snapped at him, "Close the door."

Suddenly she slammed the receiver down and glared at it in disbelief. "He lost them!" she exclaimed quietly. "He lost *all* of them! He could be anywhere by now."

Suddenly everything else fled from Chris's thoughts and he leaned across the desk and demanded tightly, "How long ago did he give them the slip?"

"Three hours ago."

"That would be shortly after my plane landed at Palma," Chris muttered. "Damn!" Thrusting his hands angrily into his pockets, he whirled to pace the room again but stopped as his fingers encountered a small piece of paper. He took it out and read the phone number where he'd reached Colette earlier that afternoon. What if Colette hadn't been kidnapped while en route to the dig? What if Roig had been holding a gun on her to force her to send Chris up there so Jondalitx could dispatch him?

"If phone numbers are as easy to trace as you claim, then this might tell us where Roig was at four o'clock this afternoon," he said, handing Eva the scrap of paper.

She gazed at it in astonishment. "You spoke to him?"

"No, I spoke to Colette Vaubois. But the chances are excellent that she was already his prisoner when I returned her call."

"It's certainly worth a try," Eva agreed. "I'll have the number traced."

A few moments later she had written an address below the phone number on the piece of paper in front of her, but she was shaking her head as she hung up the receiver.

"It's a pay phone on the docks," she said. "I'm afraid that isn't much help."

"Maybe it is," Chris contradicted her with growing excitement as a series of associations clicked in his mind. "The second time I talked to Roig in Ibiza, we met on an old boat moored to a marker buoy in the harbor. I had to rent a rowboat to get out there, but there was no sign of Roig's dinghy anywhere around."

Eva shrugged. "So? He had somebody else row him out there."

"That's not my point. If you were looking for someone and you saw this nondescript old boat tied up in the middle of nowhere with no smaller boats around, wouldn't you assume at first glance that it was empty—especially if it had been there for some time?"

Cocking her head thoughtfully, she began to nod. "You could be right, Laval. Especially if Roig only wanted to buy a little time and not hide out there permanently. I'll get right on it."

As she reached for the telephone Chris moved to the door and listened. There was still a heated discussion going on in the living room, although he couldn't make out any of the words. But Dolores seemed to be doing more of the talking than Esteban, and that was encouraging.

"All right, thanks," Eva said, and hung up the receiver. "It's all set up," she told Chris. "Two police boats with some of our operatives aboard will converge on the boat in an hour."

"What?" Chris said, dismayed. "But we may not have that much time. If Jondalitx was supposed to call in after disposing of me, then Roig knows his plan has failed. He may decide to get rid of Colette and try to run for it."

"I'm sorry, Mr. Laval, but it's going to take time to gather our agents, and we're the ones with the authority to arrest him—not the local police."

"Then *you* can take him into custody, right?" Chris pointed out excitedly.

"Yes, but it will still take a good half hour to get a taxi up here . . ." she started to explain.

"No, it won't," Chris declared emphatically.

"But how . . . ?"

"Don't ask questions, just follow me on your bike into Santa Eulalia."

"You're sure you have a plan?"

"Foolproof!" he declared. "Come on."

As they padded down the hall, Eva stopped suddenly and whispered, "Wasn't that Dolores in the living room? I wonder what she's doing here."

"Clearing up an old misunderstanding," Chris replied cryptically, and pulled her toward the front door.

Chapter 14

The taxicab was parked on the main street around the corner from the doctor's house.

"Mr. Laval, what are you doing?" Eva protested as he threw both their bikes into the backseat. "You can't just drive off in somebody else's car!"

"I don't intend to." Glancing around, he spotted the cab driver emerging from the drugstore up the street with a newspaper under his arm and waved urgently to him.

The driver broke out in smiles. By now accustomed to the style of this unusual but highly lucrative fare, he raced back to the car and got in. "Where to, *señor*?"

"I'll pay you double if you can get us to the marina in Ibiza in less than fifteen minutes," Chris told him.

"*Si, señor!*"

It was a ride a daredevil would have envied. Weaving at breakneck speed in and out of traffic on the main road into Ibiza, the driver laughed each time another vehicle had to swerve to avoid a collision. He answered the angry shouts of other motorists with rude gestures and improbable suggestions concerning their parentage. The several times that Chris glanced at Eva he found her staring tensely at the road straight ahead of them and wondered whether she was in shock. She had every right to be—the cab driver seemed to think they were all indestructible. Nonetheless he got the desired result, covering the eleven miles in ten minutes flat and dropping them off at the marina ahead of the raid party.

"I think we ought to recruit that man," Eva remarked shakily as Chris helped her out of the car.

Together they walked out to the end of the pier nearest the channel. The setting sun was spilling pink and gold into the water of the bay, and splashing all the hues of an artist's palette across the Mediterranean sky. Set against this glorious display of color like an insect crawling over a painting, the old cruiser bobbed peacefully beside the marker buoy, not even tightening its mooring-line.

The boat looked absolutely deserted, and for a split second Chris was torn by doubt. What if there was nobody aboard? Worse still, what if the concentration of police firepower at this spot enabled Roig to make good his escape from another part of the island?

"Come on," Chris said with sudden resolve. "We're going to steal a boat." He took Eva's arm and hurried her back along the pier.

"You mean borrow, don't you?"

"There's no time for semantics. We're going to take one of these rowboats and go out for a closer look at that cruiser," he told her tightly.

They skirted the channel marker and approached the larger craft on its seaward side, shipping the oars and letting their dinghy glide silently alongside. For several seconds they strained to hear some human sound from the cruiser. Then Eva shook her head and whispered, "I don't think there's anyone...conscious on board."

Noting her tactful choice of words, Chris smiled grimly to himself as he assessed the trim of the vessel. Her bow was riding quite low in the water, a clear indication that someone had either filled her fuel tank or added ballast since Chris's last meeting here with Roig.

Quickly Chris gauged the height of the deck and decided he couldn't board at the bow end. He'd have to get around to the stern, where he'd be visible from the cabin door. Blast! Indicating by gestures that they had to turn the rowboat around, Chris took one of the oars and unshipped the other for Eva to use as a paddle.

Interminable minutes later they reached the other end of the cruiser, and Chris stood up carefully in the dinghy and pulled himself as quietly as he could onto the larger vessel's sloping deck. He froze for a moment, anticipating some reaction from inside the cabin from the gentle rocking of the cruiser, and when there was none he approached the door and cautiously opened it.

A violent contrast to the ugly, utilitarian exterior of the cruiser, its interior was richly furnished, lacking few of the comforts and amenities. Chris saw a leather-and-brass bar in one corner of a cabin where mahogany and teak shone softly around hand-worked pillows and plump, brocaded seat cushions. A narrow corridor faced the door, probably leading to the galley and sleeping quarters, and Chris imagined they'd be just as well-appointed.

"Well, Mr. Laval, I see you've found me." Chris stiffened as Roig's voice drifted casually over his shoulder. He turned slowly and saw Roig standing in the doorway of a wood-finished washroom, apparently drying his hands in a thick green towel. Then the towel slid aside, revealing the cold gleam of a gun barrel trained on Chris's midriff. "You've come at a bad time," said Roig with a thin smile. "I was just leaving."

"I'll *bet* you were," retorted Chris. "Where's Colette Vaubois?"

"Huh-uh," Roig chided him. "I have the gun. I'll ask the questions. Who else knows you're here?"

"You mean who else suspects *you're* here," Chris corrected him, stalling for time till the police arrived. Now if he could just keep Roig from discovering that Eva was waiting outside!

"It's the same question," Roig snapped, waving the gun impatiently. "Just answer it!"

Sure, thought Chris, *why not! Who'd believe it anyway?*

With a perfectly straight face he replied, "Spanish Intelligence and the entire Ibizan police force."

Roig shook his head sadly. "Really, Mr. Laval, I'm disappointed in you, trying a bluff like that. I know Spanish Intelligence, and they would never let a civilian lead one of their operations."

"You're right," Chris confessed with a sheepish smile. "I should have known I couldn't fool you." Where the hell were those police boats?

"I really wish I didn't have to...terminate our association," Roig sighed. "You can be insanely courageous at times, and you seem to have phenomenal luck. You've been very hard to kill, at any rate. But please don't fancy yourself as my adversary—

you're just one of my recruits who's rebelled. You aren't the first and you won't be the last."

Keep him talking, Chris thought. *Got to keep him talking until the damn police arrive. . . .*

Aloud, he said, "And I'll bet I'm not the first you've tried to kill, either."

Roig looked puzzled for a moment. "Oh, I see," he said at last. "You'd like me to confess all my crimes to you just before someone arrives in the nick of time to save you, the way it's done in the movies. If I had the time I might humor you, Mr. Laval. But the villains in the movies are usually very vain and a little on the psychotic side, and I am neither, you see. So we'll have no true confessions this evening."

Roig glanced at his watch. Suddenly his forehead corrugated into a frown. "I really am late," he went on. "Please forgive me for rushing you, but I've planted a bomb on this boat, and I would like to get away before it goes off. If it's any consolation to you, Mr. Laval, you and your girlfriend will be dying together, like Romeo and Juliet. Turn around, please."

"Drop your gun, Roig!" came an authoritative voice from the cabin doorway.

Comprehension flashed across Roig's face then, curling his lip and hardening the expression in his eyes to cold disdain. In that instant he whirled and fired two rounds through the empty door. And a split second later, while his back was still turned, Chris picked up one of the elegant teak chairs and round-housed him with it. There was an audible crack as the chairleg connected with Roig's left arm, sending him sprawling to the floor and his gun skittering out onto the deck. "My arm," he gasped. "You broke my arm. . . ."

Suddenly Bertoldo was in the doorway, holding a pistol on Roig and glancing anxiously at Chris. "Are you all right?"

"We have to find Colette," Chris told him urgently. "Roig's planted a bomb on board."

Bertoldo scowled threateningly at the now-helpless traitor. "When does it go off, Roig? How much time have we got to find the girl?"

"Go to hell," Roig hissed.

"Where is she?" Chris demanded, his fists clenching and unclenching with helpless rage, but Roig just laughed.

As three other agents arrived to transfer the prisoner to one of the police boats, Bertoldo murmured, "We'll have to get everyone clear, Laval. You understand."

Chris was opening his mouth to protest when it suddenly dawned on him what the boat's altered trim might mean. "I think the bomb's down below, near the fuel tank," he said. "I'll bet that's where Colette is, too." Clapping Bertoldo on the arm, Chris said, "Give me three minutes, okay?"

"Three minutes," Bertoldo agreed reluctantly. "Not a second more."

Chris lifted the hatch at the prow of the cruiser and dropped lightly into the darkness of the hold. The area belowdecks smelled so strongly of kerosene that he didn't dare light a match. Damn! And he hadn't thought to bring a flashlight. As he groped his way toward the stern, the fumes wafting around him were making him nauseated and light-headed, until he was afraid he might be overcome and pass out right next to Colette. Other terrible doubts assailed him: what if he were wrong about her being down here! He hadn't even looked in the cabin's sleeping quarters. What if she were lying unconscious right above him? His three minutes were nearly up. What if he found Colette and then they had nowhere to escape to because Bertoldo had gotten everyone clear?

Suddenly he was clutching a handful of cotton fabric. Then his trembling hands located arms and legs, and a fall of soft hair.

Colette, my darling! Thank God!

Time was running out. They had to get out of there before the bomb went off. Chris was weakend by the fumes, but he still managed to lift her into his arms and make his way unsteadily back toward the dim illumination coming through the hatch. Suddenly he heard a hissing sound, and all at once the hold was filled with the flickering light of flames as fire began to dance around them, spreading rapidly along the trails of spilled kerosene.

The fuel tank was the bomb, a bomb with a dozen fuses, and they'd all just been lit. Added to the kerosene fumes in the hold, a thick pall of black smoke billowed suffocatingly around Chris as he turned in confusion, trying to rediscover the square of faint light that meant survival for him and the woman he loved.

"Laval! This way! Follow my voice!"

It was Bertoldo. Although himself gagging on the clouds of smoke rising through the hatch, he kept calling encouragement to Chris, guiding him toward the opening and finally reaching down to help him up the rungs of the metal ladder.

A small motor launch had tied up to the ladder Bertoldo had thrown over the side earlier. There were no other vessels in sight. After handing Colette down to the agent waiting in the launch, Chris and Bertoldo scrambled down the ladder. Moments later they were racing toward the police dock, glancing curiously over their shoulders at the column of smoke rising from what looked like a derelict yacht in the middle of the harbor.

As they were slowing for the approach to the crowded dock, a sound like muffled thunder erupted behind them, and they turned to see Roig's boat going up in flames.

"Three minutes was just about right," Chris commented, a little awestruck by the force of the explosion.

"It would have been," was Bertoldo's calm reply. "You took five."

Just then Colette stirred, and Chris placed a comforting arm around her shoulders. "It's all right, darling," he crooned. "You're going to be all right now."

"Mmm... Chris?" she murmured faintly. "I'm sorry, Chris. I didn't want to say those things to you over the phone, but he made me and then he forced me to drink something...." Suddenly sobs wracked her body and she was weeping uncontrollably against his shoulder.

Chris held her tightly, not wanting to move, never wanting to let her go for the rest of his life. The nightmare was finally over.

"I love you, Colette," he whispered fervently into her ear. "And I'm going to protect you. Nobody will ever harm you again."

Not even the gathering darkness of nightfall could disguise the adoring look in her eyes as they met his.

"I loved you from the first time we talked, on the ship from Barcelona," she murmured. "I set my cap for you that night."

The love on their lips as they met in a kiss tasted a little like smoke.

Chapter 15

"What shall we toast?" Esteban asked, raising his glass of *rumani* into the air and pausing expectantly.

"How about the end of one counterespionage career?" suggested Dolores, with a smile that showed clearly how little she regretted giving it up.

"Better make that two counterespionage careers," Chris corrected her as all four of them broke into laughter.

Esteban gestured for silence. "To a future filled with love and happiness for us all," he said, and everyone nodded and touched glasses. "Christopher, I hope that you and Colette will be able to help Dolores and me celebrate our wedding in June."

Chris gazed into Colette's radiant face. "We'd be delighted," he said, "provided you two will come to our ceremony in the fall."

"That's a deal," Dolores said happily.

Suddenly there was a knock at Esteban's front door, and the conversation was suspended while Soledad went to see who it was. A moment later Eva Tirso appeared in the living room door, smiling shyly.

"I'm sorry to disturb you," she apologized, reaching into her purse, "but we discovered that Mr. Laval and Miss Vaubois were leaving tomorrow morning for Paris, and the bureau wanted me to convey their deepest gratitude to you both for the part you played in putting an end to Fernando Roig's spy ring. Your courage on Monday evening was especially remarkable, Mr. Laval. We'd like you to have this." And she handed him a small bronze medal on a blue ribbon.

Everyone clapped as Chris accepted the medal with a flushed face. "Thanks," he said with a smile. "Can you tell me something, though?"

"If I can."

"How was Roig planning to escape from his boat that night? I've been thinking and thinking about that, and it's driving me crazy."

"On Roig's signal, one of his associates was going to make a circuit of the bay in a motor launch and pick him up. It would have worked, except that one of our people recognized the associate as he loitered on the dock and arrested him."

"Then Roig was lucky to get away with just a broken arm," Chris remarked. Eva just smiled. "All right, here's another question that's been nagging me—who staged the art theft at the *casa*, and why?"

This time Dolores answered. "Spanish Intelligence did—only it wasn't really an art theft. You see, they'd known about Roig's connection with Diego, then later they saw Roig contact Esteban—that was when it was decided to put him under surveillance." She glanced lovingly at the count. "Sorry, darling. I only found out about all this recently. I promise you that when I was following orders, I didn't know *you* were under suspicion."

Esteban smiled. "Don't worry about that now. It's all over and done with, thank God."

"But where did I come in?" Chris persisted.

"Flatlander," Colette murmured. "You'll have to tie up all the loose ends for him or we'll never get any peace."

Dolores laughed. "Apparently the surveillance of Esteban was turning up a big fat zero, so they decided to see if they could panic him into making a false move. Roig had sometimes used art works to conceal his shipments. So we took the opportunity of staging that art "theft" and making sure you, Chris, witnessed it. I guess my superiors thought that when Chris told Esteban about it, he'd immediately jump to the conclusion that Roig was up to something—without telling him . . . especially when he learned that nothing had been taken, and a woman fitting my description was involved."

Dolores paused, as she walked over to the count and put her hand in his. "Of course, Esteban, being innocent, did not contact Roig. . . . "

"So they turned their attention to me," Chris murmured. "You know, I shudder to think what would have happened to you *had* I been one of Roig's boys. I might have told him about the incident and described you to him. He'd have smelled a rat immediately."

Dolores shrugged. "I suppose it was a calculated risk."

"My God," Esteban groaned.

Eva broke into the conversation briskly. "Well, now all that's settled. By the way," she added, turning to Dolores, "before Roig is extradited to France he'll be tried in Barcelona on the charges we discussed yesterday. Will you be available to testify?"

"Absolutely," Dolores assured her.

"Good. I'll let our Barcelona office know." The business part of the conversation over, Eva shook hands all around and said, "Mr. Laval, Miss Vaubois, have a safe and pleasant journey home." Then she bowed slightly to her former employer and left.

"I'M STILL NOT SURE what was going on," Colette confessed as they walked alone together on the beach behind her hotel. "Do you think we'll ever find out the whole story about Roig and Esteban's brother, for instance?"

"Probably not," Chris replied tranquilly. "Intelligence people tend to be rather closemouthed about ongoing operations. I have a sneaking suspicion, though, that among the charges Dolores and Eva discussed was the murder of Diego de Charraca."

"What? How did you figure that one out?"

Chris shrugged. "Oh, some deductive reasoning on my part," he said complacently.

"Hah!" Colette snorted.

"I guess we'll have to wait and see what happens at his trial."

Colette sighed. "I still can't believe we're going home tomorrow."

"It hasn't been much of a vacation, has it?" Chris agreed. "Just keep thinking about the summer, when you'll be flying to Canada with me to meet my parents, and— Oh, no!"

It was raining. Huge drops splashed down on the sand, polka-dotting it as Chris gazed helplessly toward the gray sky overhead.

"You know what I think?" Colette said wryly, "I think you're a rainmaker in disguise. If you don't leave this island I think it's going to rain here for forty days and forty nights."

"Not on us, it isn't!" Chris declared, pulling her toward the line of cabanas that rimmed the beach.

Once inside the little cubicle, Chris sat down and drew Colette onto his lap. Once again her nearness was intoxicating. But this time he could revel in her fragrant softness, in the inviting curves of her body, in the sweetness of her lips, and give her in return the strength of his arms and the boldness of his passion, without fear or restraint. For in their shared kiss was the shared promise of a life spent loving and learning together.

4 FREE

MYSTIQUE BOOKS
Your FREE gift includes . . .

Exciting novels of romance, suspense and drama, with intriguing characters and surprising plot twists, set against international backgrounds.

PROPER AGE FOR LOVE, *Claudette Jaunière*

Anne didn't understand when her fiancé suggested she become his mistress — not his wife. And so she fled across Europe into a nightmare of intrigue and danger where her very survival depended on the man she most loved — and feared.

ISLAND OF DECEIT, *Alix André*

Determined to discover her sister's fate on an exotic Caribbean isle, Rosalie finds herself enmeshed in a web of lies, dangerously attracted to the only man who might know the dreadful truth.

HIGH WIND IN BRITTANY, *Caroline Gayet*

What elaborate charade of identity was the stranger playing on the tiny coastal town? Only Marie knew, and her knowledge brought her danger.

HOUSE OF SECRETS, *Denise Noël*

Would Pascale reveal a family secret kept hidden for years . . . or stand accused of murdering another woman to protect the man she loved?

Your FREE gift includes

House of Secrets—by Denise Noël
Proper Age for Love—by Claudette Jaunière
Island of Deceit—by Alix André
High Wind in Brittany—by Caroline Gayet

Mail this coupon today!

FREE GIFT CERTIFICATE
and Subscription Reservation

Mail this coupon today.
To: Mystique Books

In U.S.A.
M.P.O. Box 707
Niagara Falls, NY 14302

In Canada
649 Ontario Street
Stratford, Ontario, M5A 6W2

Please send me my 4 Mystique Books **free.**
Also, reserve a subscription to the 4 NEW
Mystique Books published each month. Each
month I will receive 4 NEW Mystique Books at
the low price of $1.50 [total $6.00 a month].

There are no shipping and handling nor any
other hidden charges. I may cancel this
arrangement at any time, but even if I do, these
first 4 books are still mine to keep.

My present
membership
number is

NAME   (PLEASE PRINT)

ADDRESS

CITY   STATE/PROV.   ZIP/POSTAL CODE

Offer not valid for present Mystique subscribers.
Offer expires August 31, 1980.
Prices subject to change without notice.

00256456200